Call Me Blessed

Call Me Blessed

JOHN L. BRESKA

RESOURCE *Publications* · Eugene, Oregon

CALL ME BLESSED

Resource Publications
An Imprint of Wipf and Stock Publishers
199 W. 8th Ave., Suite 3
Eugene, OR 97401

www.wipfandstock.com

PAPERBACK ISBN: 979-8-3852-2405-0
HARDCOVER ISBN: 979-8-3852-2406-7
EBOOK ISBN: 979-8-3852-2407-4

06/26/24

Alcoholics Anonymous, Author: Alcoholics Anonymous World Services, Inc.

Scripture quotations are from Revised Standard Version of the Bible, copyright © 1946, 1952, and 1971 National Council of the Churches of Christ in the United States of America. Used by permission. All rights reserved worldwide.

To GOD, who created everything.
To Jesus Christ our LORD and Savior.
To Peter, Patrick, and Michael, along with those many other children I
shared my childhood with including my sister, Judith.

Contents

Introduction

THESE STORIES TOOK SEED some years ago. Over the seasons, I've watered and weeded them, that they might be read and realized. In each story there are several lessons that could be applied in life and hopefully make life a bit easier as one moves along. I share these stories, hoping the values of our society do not crumble, and GOD's Way might be preserved.

The Gate

DEIDRA WAS A QUIET, thought filled child who was often taken for slow-witted or distant. Distant perhaps but slow-witted was not the case. She was a deep thinker with a strong spiritual side to her and that made her different. The children her age could be cruel and often picked on her for her strange ways and mannerisms. She came from a single parent home where her father took care of her. Deidra's mother had passed away from cervical cancer a little bit more than five years earlier when she was seven years old. This was reasoned by many of her teachers as the cause for her distant and peculiar behavior. The truth was that Deidra saw the world differently. Her father worked long hours in a machine shop, milling parts for various machine assembly lines and assorted equipment. He made a decent living, but it drained him of the skills needed to be both father and mother to Deidra.

Many times, after preparing and eating their supper, Deidra's dad would fall into a hard asleep in the large living room recliner. She would clean up the kitchen and take care of the leftovers after he dozed off. When Deidra finished tidying up the kitchen, she would do her homework, then wake her father to let him know it was time for bed and that he should lock up the house for the night.

They lived on a twenty-acre parcel of land which had been willed to Harvey Hold, her father, by her grandparents Louise and Earnest Hold. Deidra loved to play around the outbuildings and fields surrounding the old farmhouse. In the past, her grandparents owned over one hundred acres, but sold some off as the years progressed to keep debt from their backdoor. Farming was a lost art, and mega farms became the large producers, making it hard for the little independent farmer to make a living. The need for the acreage faded along with farm life. Today the land had gone back to being wild. Harvey maintained a large garden, giving much to the food bank in town yet, keeping enough for the two of them.

Deidra was categorized as a loner by her peers. Her peculiar or quiet behavior kept many of her classmates away from her. Her fellow classmates had given her, in so many words, their permission to be part of the nerd table but Deidra marched to a different drummer and did not care. She would not be part of their group or clique but instead, followed her own path. Refusing to become part of the gang, she opted to be by herself and that left her with few friends. Most of her peers were pressured by others to stay away from her. Such is the nature of people who do not understand another's ways. She was always pleasant even when somebody was downright mean to her. Many thought she was too dull to understand when they were insulting her, but the reality of it all was, that she would not play into their behavioral traps.

One boy took this all in from a distance. He found Deidra intriguing and was drawn to her. He too suffered the loss of a parent, but his loss was recent. His father died in a freak accident about two months earlier. He had stepped off a curb and was crossing a street by slipping between two parked cars. Upon reaching the street, he was hit and killed by a man on a motorcycle who came out of nowhere. This happened on a business trip to Denver, three hundred miles south of home. When this news reached the young man and his mother, their life was shattered. They were both still in the process of picking up the pieces, to make their new life work without the head of the family.

The reality hadn't quite sunk in yet, that Dad was not coming home. As far as Peter was concerned, his father was still away, even though he experienced the funeral and burial. Denial was such a strong force in the boy's young mind.

After many days of watching Deidra, Peter decided to approach her. There were times where he had wanted to step between her and the others to protect her, when those kids were giving her the business. Sadly, he felt helpless with his own issues he was dealing with and not confident at all. He found himself following her home one day after school, when she turned suddenly and said, "Would you like to walk with me?"

Peter approached her and when they were eye to eye he said, "I'd like to know you."

"Well, c'mon then. I'm Deidra Hold, and you are?"

"I know," Peter replied.

"Nice to meet you, I know," and they both laughed. It was the first time Peter laughed since his father's passing. It felt like a weight had been removed from his chest.

"You know they'll pick on you for being my friend," she offered, then added, "They pick on me all the time. It's a shame they can't get past themselves."

Peter wondered what Deidra meant by that but didn't question it. He just walked along with her until they got to her house on the edge of town.

"What's your name?" she asked a second time when they got to her front yard.

"Peter, Peter Lacy. Sorry, I thought you were good with I know," and they laughed again as she said goodbye.

"Hope we get to chat again," she said, as she went up the walk to her house.

Peter turned down the road and headed back in the direction of his house, which was in town. He knew he was going to be late but would explain that he met a friend. Mom worried about him overtime, mostly because of the loss of his father. Peter knew that and tried to get her not to worry but he figured she'd get better in time.

Less possessive and all that, he thought.

As he made his way back to his house, Peter saw the neighbor's dog, Roscoe, heading for the field down the road. The dog disappeared in the tall weeds as the boy mused, *Someone left the gate open!*

Focusing back on his problem, he was ready for his mother's panicked face when he walked in the door. She would be happy to hear that he was talking to someone, anyone his age that might pull him out of the depression she was observing. It was apparent in herself as well. She would still be upset at him for being late.

She was waiting on the porch when Peter arrived. Quickly she asked, "Are you OK? You're late Peter! I was worried. Is everything alright?"

"Yes Mom, I'm fine. I met a new friend and walked her home," Peter explained.

"You walked HER home? You're only twelve Peter. A bit young to have a girlfriend, don't you think?" Mom chattered.

"Almost thirteen and it's not like that, Mom. We just met and started talking. She's nice and could use a friend. So could I, for that matter." Peter finished and went to the bathroom to wash up for supper.

When he returned to the kitchen table, his mother was filling his plate with green beans, macaroni and cheese, and a well-done burger. She looked up and asked, "Well, are you going to tell me her name, Peter?"

"Oh sure! It's Deidra Hold, Mom," Peter shared.

"I think I've heard of that girl. Isn't she the one . . . they . . . ?"

"Don't, Mom! She's not odd. She's just . . . Deidra, that's all. I find that she doesn't follow the pack and she has a kind side to her too!" Peter concluded, as he began eating his supper.

The next day Peter looked for Deidra at school. When he finally caught up to her, she was cornered next to the lockers with Josie and Becky picking on her about something. When Peter walked up to the three of them in the hallway, Josie said, "So is this the boyfriend? He's a geek!"

"Well, he is a boy, and he is my friend," she said to Josie then looked at Peter and asked, "You are my friend, right?"

"Yes, I'm your friend. What's going on here?" Peter questioned.

"It's none of your business, friend," Josie shot back.

Peter replied, "Listen, why don't you just leave Deidra alone. She's never done anything to you."

Out of nowhere came an older boy's voice asking, "Are you picking on my sister?" which was followed by a punch in the right eye, by a fourteen-year-old that was in the eighth grade. This was Josie's older brother and self-appointed tough guy, Fred.

Blam! Peter hit the floor grabbing his face.

"That was a terrible thing to do," Deidra shouted at Fred Mueller.

"Back off or you'll get the same weirdo," Fred barked with his hand in a fist.

"Go ahead if it makes you feel more superior, Fred Mueller," Deidra answered calmly, regaining her composure.

Just then the bell rang, signaling that lunch was over and so was the boxing round. The teachers and other students emptied the cafeteria while Peter was getting back up on his feet. Peter's teacher walked up and asked what was going on, to which Peter replied, "Sorry, Mrs. Albright. I ran into Fred, not watching where I was going." Peter saw that Deidra was going to interject, but he waved her off with a look as to say, just let it go.

Fred made a quick exit behind his sister and her friend Becky, mingling in with the other students. Within five minutes time, everyone was back in their classrooms and life went on.

The two friends met outside the school after the school day was completed. By then Peter was sporting a nice shiner.

"Did you go to the nurse?" Deidra asked.

"No. I'm OK. Let's just forget about the whole thing."

"Thanks for coming to my aid, Peter. They never quit. It's always something. I don't know how they found out so quickly that we had talked yesterday." Deidra said, as they started on their way toward her house.

"You don't have to walk me home, you know."

"I know, but I want to walk you home. I like you," Peter explained, as he smiled and winced at the same time.

"When we get to my house, we're going to put some ice on that. Maybe the swelling will come down, so your mom doesn't have a fit."

"OK . . . might be a good idea," Peter replied, as he thought about his mom and one hundred questions when he got home.

The two were both kind of quiet after that last exchange and just walked for a while. Peter looked frustrated, as well as angry most of the walk to Deidra's house.

Deidra finally decided to share something when they approached her house. She stopped walking, then turned toward her new friend saying, "After we fix your eye, I want to show you something."

The boy's eyes kind of lit up as his imagination wandered, then Deidra continued, "It's out in the field. I guess you could say it's a very special place. Come on inside and let's help that eye out," she said, with a soft smile that lit up the boy's heart.

She had dark raven hair and the palest of blue eyes. Deidra was several inches shorter than Peter. An average girl in weight meaning she was neither heavy nor thin and if one was to rate her beauty, it was something that rose from her inner depths. She emitted a peace that shone like the colors in a flower. At twelve years old, all the telltale signs of her blossoming into a lovely young lady were there.

The two entered the house and Deidra told Peter to grab a kitchen chair. She went to the refrigerator to gather some ice in a plastic container. Deidra got a hand towel out and placed five cubes in the cloth. Wrapping it up, she made sure it was secure.

"Here . . . this should help," she said, as she handed Peter the freshly packaged ice cubes and sat down across from him.

"What are you thinking about Deidra?" Peter asked, as she stared at him.

"I've never shared my place out back with anyone. I was looking at you to make sure I was making the right decision," she said point blank.

"And . . .?" he questioned.

Deidra blossomed into a wide smile and said, "Yes! You are the one I'll share my secret with."

The sound of tires on gravel told of a vehicle coming up the driveway. It was Deidra's father coming home after work.

"Well, what do we have here?" Deidra's father asked with a questioning face, as he entered the backdoor.

"This is Peter, Dad. I guess you could say he came to my aid when some of my classmates were giving me a hard time. He took a shot to the eye for me, so I let him walk me home," then she laughed, which only increased the puzzled look on her father's face.

"Nice to meet you, Mr. Hold," Peter said, standing and extending his hand. "It really wasn't that big a deal and Deidra offered me some ice for my eye," Peter stumbled with his words, as Deidra's father shook the boy's hand.

"Well, it's nice to meet you, Peter. Nasty shiner! It's nice that Deidra has a friend, but I don't like you kids fighting. I'm going to shower then get supper cooking, Deidra. Don't forget you have homework to do," which was her father's way of saying to the boy not to hang around too long.

"I won't, Dad. We're going to go out back for a little bit, then Peter needs to get home," she responded, letting her father know she had a plan.

Mr. Hold left the kitchen for other parts of the house and the two kids slipped out of the back screen door. The late September skies were clear and had that beginning of harvest time in the air. The air smelled good.

"Come around here. There's a path behind the shed," Deidra pointed out.

Peter followed like a puppy. He really liked Deidra. She was different but in such a good way. She was, like his mom would say, refreshing. They walked down the path past a few trees, then out into the open field where wildflowers, thistles, and other plants that grew out of the unattended land took hold. After they cleared one field that was bordered by a barbwire fence, they slipped through the wire very carefully. They then passed several oaks and there it was, just before the forest began.

It was a gate, but what struck Peter as strange was, it wasn't attached to a fence. It had an eight-inch round vertical post, which was flat on top and set into the ground. There was another post on the other side of the gate that was the same. In between the posts was a hinged gate made from pieces of two-inch rough, rounded oak. All the wood had been debarked. The hinges were made of iron attached to the one post. They were rusted from age. *The gate looked old, like it had been there for maybe one hundred years or more,* the boy thought, processing what he was seeing. It had been constructed well, even though it was weathered from the elements and time.

Peter noticed that the path stopped abruptly at the gate. Oddly, there was no worn path on the other side. He started to walk around the gate to observe it from the other side, but Deidra called him back.

"You can't get to the other side from there," she explained. "You have to go through the gate," and she smiled that comforting smile she wore.

Peter looked puzzled at her instructions but cast it off as just being Deidra. He walked back and stood next to her while she unfastened the clasp which held the gate closed. She struggled at first with the rusty clasp and pin. Peter helped her and it gave way, sliding back. The hinges creaked as she pushed the gate open toward the other side. Peter followed directly behind her, and as they walked into the field, he felt an overwhelming sensation of something from another place.

"I feel angelic!" he shouted. It was as if he was being washed inside and out from all worry, fear, depression, and anxiety. All of that was replaced with a joy that transcended happiness at any level he had previously known.

He fell to the ground amazed by this happening, looking toward Deidra in total awe. She too was feeling it, but seemed to handle it better, as she had been there before. Deidra walked over to Peter, extending a hand to help him back to his feet. When they both were standing, she said, "I feel my mother's presence here. I believe it's a gate that opens to heaven or someplace close to heaven, Peter."

"I . . . I think you might be right Deidra. I have this peace that my father's in a good place and he's happy, yet, he still feels distant to me. I'm feeling lightheaded from all of this."

"OK, we can go for now and maybe come back another time," Deidra suggested.

"Who built this?" Peter asked, as they turned toward the house.

"My grandfather's father built this, as I understand the story. It was after my great grandmother passed. Dad says there was a small fenced in area originally, but everything fell back to the earth over time, except for the gate. He thinks maybe my great grandmother is buried out here somewhere. We looked a few times for a marker but never did find one."

The two retraced their steps, which were no more than a dozen or so, and closed the gate behind them. Peter walked around the gate to the other side checking it out, for the boy's curiosity had been raised. There was no strange feeling nor mystical surge as he had felt when they went through the gate. And still, they both felt that they had traveled much farther than a dozen steps.

"Has your dad been down here?"

"Not recently, but he did come a few times after my mom passed away. He doesn't feel it like we did," Deidra responded. "Maybe it's an age thing," she added.

As they returned to her house, Peter exclaimed, "I never felt like that before today. In fact, I was downright sick over my father's passing and haven't talked to anyone about my father since he's been gone. It's a nice feeling to know he's in a good place."

When Deidra and Peter approached her house, Peter added, "I better get home Deidra. My mom's going to have a fit."

With that, Peter took off in the direction of his house. Fifteen minutes later, he walked in through the backdoor. He was better than an hour late, which was earmarked by the cold plate of food sitting on the table. His mother waited quietly in the living room for his explanation.

Walking into the room he said, "I'm sorry, Mom. I lost track of the time."

"What on earth happened to your eye, young man?" his mother blurted out when she saw the shiner he was sporting.

"I fell down in gym, Mom. It's no big deal," Peter lied to keep the questioning minimized and it made him uncomfortable.

"I understand the eye, but not calling? I'm sure there is a phone at this girl's house. You were with that girl I'm guessing. Consider yourself grounded for a week," his mother directed in a calm distant voice.

"I want you home directly after school for the rest of the week. No negotiations until then. Am I understood?"

"Yes, Mom, and yes, I was at Deidra's," Peter replied, and went to his room without eating, which was entirely his choice. It was there that he brooded for a time, not because he was grounded, as he felt he deserved it, but because he would not get to see his newfound friend. Lying to his mother also gnawed on him.

As he sat at his desk in his bedroom, starting to work on his homework, he realized he had not argued about the punishment, which was a first for him. Peter knew he was wrong and knew he could have called, but he was inconsiderate and accepted the punishment without a fuss. He wondered if his experience at the gate had anything to do with his attitude. Telling the lie made him feel very uncomfortable. Finally, after five days passed, he told his mother he got in a fight of sorts. After some back and forth dialogue with his parent, the boy felt much better.

He felt like changes within him had taken place. They were good changes that gave him solace, as he had been in a state of major depression. Somehow, what happened had brought light to the loss of his father. This bit of gloom would soon be over. Peter made a mental note not to get into this kind of situation again. It was only the right behavior to follow.

The rest of the week went by slowly, as does any period of time when constraints are put on a person. Peter got to see Deidra in school, but they only had time to chat during lunch. After they walked through the cafeteria line for their meal, they would search each other out. Then the two of them would find a corner table so they could talk. Sometimes they were joined by a few of the less popular kids. Other days they were alone but not without being hassled by the girls who gave Deidra a hard time in the hall the week before.

Peter was miffed at why they were so persistent at being annoying. Josie made sure to walk by with her food tray in hand, followed by her friends, in order to make some derogatory remark as she passed. This infuriated Peter but Deidra just told him to let it go.

"They will tire of their foolishness in time," she explained.

"I know, but it ticks me off that they can't find something better to do," Peter countered, as he looked at them a few tables over from where the two friends sat.

On Friday at lunch, Fred Mueller tripped a small kid named Charlie and he fell face first into his tray of food. Fred laughed like a hyena. It was then that Peter approached Fred, but a teacher who was monitoring the cafeteria stepped between them and told them to move on, as she helped Charlie to his feet. Hard stares were cast by both boys, and it looked like trouble was brewing down the line. Peter had had just about enough of the older boy's aggressive behavior, always directed at those weaker than him. Deidra tried to explain to Peter, before classes resumed, that Fred would eventually get his due even though they might not be there to witness it. Life had a way of balancing out the good and bad, which was created by each individual. Peter seemed to understand all of this she was saying, but still wanted to sock that jerk right in the mug, to give him a taste of his own medicine.

Deidra waited after school near the tree where the two would chat briefly before each returned to their homes. However, Peter never showed up that Friday afternoon. There was no way that Deidra could have known he was called into the principal's office. He hadn't done anything wrong but rather was questioned about the lunchtime incident between Charlie Ratzar and Fred Mueller. After some coaxing, Peter explained to the principal that it was a deliberate trip by Fred. The principal, in turn, told Peter that it would be addressed and thanked him for his honesty.

After a while Deidra left their meeting place, figuring that Peter had his fill of her preaching to him about turning the other cheek. She walked her normal route home, taking the path that weaved along the river. She wondered if her "turn the other cheek" attitude was a magnet for trouble. As she moved along the path, she felt like she was being watched. Her inner hunch was correct. As she rounded a few very large trees that the path went around, there was evidence of erosion below the trees. The path Deidra was on was extremely close to the edge of the bank and lacked a guardrail. It was getting worse every year and the town needed to address it. It was a considerable drop to the waters below.

As Deidra made the turn, Josie and her two comrades were waiting for her.

"Where's your protector now, weirdo?" Josie shouted out.

"Listen . . . I'm not looking for any trouble, Josie. I really don't know what I ever did to you that you're so upset with me," Deidra responded. "Please leave me be!"

"We can't stand how uppity you think you are," Josie screamed, as she lunged forward at Deidra. Deidra pushed her back hard, with both arms. It wasn't what she had wanted to do, but it was effective enough to have the girls back off. They needed to know she had boundaries and enough was enough.

"I'm sorry I pushed you, but you just won't listen! Now leave me be please! I didn't search you out! You came to me looking for trouble and I don't want any trouble," Deidra shouted, then moved past them down the path toward her home.

Josie sat on a stump rubbing her shoulders and cursed out her two friends by saying, "Why didn't you jump that freak when she pushed me?!"

"Well, you started it, Josie. You got almost the same as her boyfriend got from your brother. We're getting kind of tired of picking on Deidra anyway," Barbara told her.

Becky also said, "Yeah, this is getting old and we're going to get in trouble. We need to find something better to do."

"You two can go choke. You're not my friends anymore," Josie screamed, as they walked away.

Saturday morning was the completion of the punishment of being grounded for a week. Peter had breakfast at the kitchen table along with his mother, who had prepared oatmeal with walnuts and a touch of honey. It was extremely quiet at the table when finally, his mother spoke.

"I hope you don't feel I was too hard on you, Peter, but your father is no longer here to give you guidance."

She began to tear up when Peter responded with, "Mom, I deserved the grounding. I was wrong not to let you know where I was. It's not going to happen again."

"What are your plans for today?" his mother asked.

"I'm going over to Deidra's house for a while. She's just a friend, Mom, and don't stare at me. I did my punishment for not letting you know where I was. Now, I'm telling you where I will be," Peter said in earnest.

"OK, fair enough. I'm going grocery shopping. Let me know if you're eating lunch over there, will you?"

Peter replied with, "Sure, Mom. I might if I'm asked, but I'll call and let you know before noon as to what's going on."

He gave her a kiss on the cheek and bounded out the backdoor. Peter's mother looked down at the table and smiled to herself. The boy's thoughts were far down the road, while his mother's thoughts were still at the table, thinking about how her son was growing up so fast. He was going to have his thirteenth birthday in spring.

While Deidra and Peter's friendship grew over the next several months, Josie found someone new to pick on to keep up her "skills." Winter arrived and departed, chock full of colorful holidays, holy days, and a New Year's Day as well. Josie eventually won back her friends by treating them to malts downtown or having them over for sleepovers. Life seemed to regain a certain balance once again.

When spring returned, Peter and Deidra would sit out on her property and talk for hours under some trees just past the shed. Sometimes they would go through the gate. When they did, they went through sparingly, for they felt it was a special place and should be treated as such.

School ended for the summer break. They were now into the magical teenage years, as each had celebrated birthdays. Their friendship grew very strong over winter into spring. On one day in mid-July, Deidra and Peter went through the gate. Overcome with the same celestial feelings, both teens dropped to their knees, equally as much in adoration, as in finding a steady hold on the ground. It was at this place and time that Peter felt a strong connection to his father. He explained it later as an understanding within of what happened to his father at the end his life. An immaculate peace and love in all things put the young boy's thoughts into perspective. Everything was good.

School started the first week of September and life flowed for a time. Fred Mueller was no longer a part of the equation, having moved on to his freshman year at the high school. Like weeds, old behaviors rose to the surface again. Josie was bent on revenge for getting shoved back by Deidra last September. She wasn't even interested in bringing her crew in on what she was planning. This was something she intended to do all by herself. *Perhaps the same punishment Fred might deliver,* she thought.

Josie was in the same grade and class that Deidra was in. The previous year they were in different classrooms throughout the day. Each grade level had two classrooms. This year Josie had opportunities to be aggravating all day long if she wanted to, but she didn't stir things up. In fact, she put on a good act of ignoring Deidra with an occasional hello. Her idea was to build up some normalcy, which would get Deidra's guard down at some place in time. Josie was a big boned girl. She was also about three inches taller than Deidra. Josie's size intimidated Deidra. Her classmate had sprouted up over winter. The new aloofness puzzled Deidra at first until it became commonplace.

Perhaps Josie has outgrown her need to annoy me, Deidra thought.

Peter had been working on an eighth-grade shop project. It was a Friday night after school classes, late October. The boy stayed in the shop class to put the final coat of varnish on a hard rock maple tray he had made for his mother. Deidra said she needed to get supper on for her father, so she couldn't wait for him to finish, or she would be late. They both agreed to Peter visiting on Saturday. The two could go fishing down by the river or Planter's Lake which was about a mile from Deidra's house. They had a date, although the word date was not to be used in front of Peter's mom or Deidra's father.

Around 6 p.m. Deidra's father called Peter's house and talked, first to Peter's mother then to Peter. Deidra had not come home yet, and he wondered if she was visiting over there. When everyone realized she was missing, the police were called. By mid-Saturday many in the town realized they had a missing girl from their area and several small search parties combed the river and two wooded areas near town's outskirts. The police even took the time to search Planter's Lake with a dive team. There was no one to be found nor any evidence giving the authorities some type of lead. It was as if Deidra had just vanished.

Four days had passed without a sign of her. Peter was sick with worry. The police had questioned him twice, as he was her closest friend. They continued to check the river area as well as the lake again, fearing she might have fallen in. There was also speculation of abduction, but there was nothing to go on in any direction. The authorities were coming up empty.

Peter rose from his bed the morning of the fifth day with an idea. The young man called Mr. Hold on the telephone to ask if he might come over and search the areas where he and Deidra would spend hours talking. Even though Deidra's father and others had checked the area, Peter wanted another look. He wanted Mr. Hold to be aware that he was on his property.

When Peter arrived at the Hold's property, Mr. Hold said, "Anything you can think of that might help me find my daughter is fine with me, Peter." One could visibly see the worry on Deidra's father's face and in his posture.

Within twenty minute's time, Peter walked around the side of the house beyond the shed and followed the path across the acreage to where the oaks stood. He paused there for a few minutes, remembering their laughter and more serious times when they shared their feelings about the loss of their parents.

Peter looked past the trees to where the old gate stood a hundred feet away. He moved in the direction of the strange phenomena. When he got to the gate, he unlatched it, then opened it carefully and walked through. Once again, he was taken almost off his feet by the light feeling. He had entered into a place which was filled with the Spirit of that which makes everything a reality.

When he was in this place, there were never any worries upon his heart. This time was different. He felt an odd feeling, which was like the very first time he had entered with Deidra. It was like he knew of his father and that his father was safe, except this time his feelings were of Deidra. It struck him in those moments that she was safe. He sat quietly for a time. As tears rolled down his cheeks, the realization came to him. It was like the second time he went through the gate and had deep feelings about his father. This time it was Deidra's spirit talking to Peter and explaining she was in a better place. That she too was safe.

An image came to Peter that Deidra's body was in the river. He began to cry out loud. Peter had lost his best friend, but now he knew where she was. He gathered himself and returned to the house so he could have Mr. Hold call the police.

"I don't know how he knows but he says he can lead you to where she is at. No . . . no, I don't think he had anything to do with it," Deidra's father said then hung up.

"Thanks, Mr. Hold," was all Peter could muster up as they waited for the police.

A couple of hours later, and around a mile down river, they found Deidra's remains. Her body had gotten lodged beneath some fallen tree branches, a sweeper they call it, which were under the water's surface. There were questions that needed to be answered after the coroner found some interesting evidence later that day.

In Deidra's right hand was a piece of material which resembled a part of a sleeve which was flowered in appearance and looked like it had been torn from a shirt, blouse, or dress. After a few days, Josie Mueller was called in for questioning, as were several other students including Peter. Peter had told the police the material looked familiar to him. He thought about it for a time, then he told the authorities he believed he saw Josie wearing something which had that floral pattern on it at school earlier in the week.

When the police had her parents bring Josie to the police station for additional questioning, they presented the piece of blouse to her and her parents. The young lady broke down crying, "It was all an accident! I never meant for it to happen," she cried.

Josie finally confessed that she had laid in waiting for Deidra along the river trail. It was her intention to even the score for the two-armed push she got the previous year from her classmate. When she surprised Deidra and a fight broke out, she pushed her too hard. Josie explained that Deidra lost her footing near the riverbank. As she fell, Deidra grabbed hold of Josie's blouse and ripped a portion of the sleeve off. Josie ran in panic back to her place, where she buried the blouse in the backyard. She thought the mishap would all go away. She hoped that the river would hide the ill deed. When she was asked why she persisted in fighting with the deceased over a couple of years, she stared blankly and said, "I don't know."

Peter lost his best friend. Josie messed up her young life, and a father lost his daughter all because of bullying. Peer pressure and foolish decisions brought a young girl's life to an end and ruined another girl's life. Peter is in his late forties now, but every so many years, he returns to the town where he grew up and visits the Hold's farm. The gate is gone and so is Deidra's father, but the new owner allows Peter a walk out by the oak trees. The owner has witnessed Peter standing about hundred feet or so, out in the middle of the field. He stands quietly for a time, with a smile on his face and a tear on his cheek, remembering.

Call Me Lucky

LOOKING BACK ON ONE's life brings both the good and bad that happened to mind. I'll do my best to be as accurate as I can, trying hard not to embellish the facts. Let me begin by stating that I am a dog.

Born third out of a litter of six, I entered the world with a wet nose and all my parts. Sporting one white paw on my left front leg, the rest of me was the color of a whitetail deer or a light brown overall. I didn't know this at the time but when I reached maturity, I would weigh out at forty-five pounds. I was a short-haired, curbstone setter which spoke of a mix of breeds, most likely from a couple of canines in our vast neighborhood. The people my mom lived with were a good family and I enjoyed the first fourteen months growing up in their house.

I can still remember my first toy, which was a couple old socks. There was one sock inside of another and several knots were tied in it. A good part of it was white but it sported a green and gray stripe around the opened end. I would shake that thing around the room until I got dizzy. Other times, one of my brothers would fight me for possession of the sock and we would end up in a pulling contest that would last until the next distraction or nap time. It was at this time that I learned to work my mouth for possession of the toy, while keeping one eye raised and focused on what was happening around me. It gave me a slightly crazy look, which helped in the defense of retaining anything that I had clamped down on.

It was a good life for the first twelve weeks, then things began to happen. One by one my siblings began to disappear. Our owners would have other people come for a short visit and the next thing I would see is one of my brothers express goodbyes with those sad puppy eyes staring back at me. My one and only sister was the first to leave. Never even got to hear the name she was given. Now that I think back to that time, I really don't remember any of their names. I remembered what they called me. I don't have a very good mental picture of how they were marked, except for one brother, who had a white ear with a brown tip. His colors I remembered. I was tempted to bite down on that tip every time I saw it. I guess that's why it stuck in my mind.

Time seems to eat holes in parts of the past while other happenings fade slowly away over the years. There also are the memories, which visit in the night to haunt the mind. These were the thoughts that make a sleeping dog shake his or her leg, whimpering at the same time over the trials and mishaps one has encountered on the trail of life. I'm still troubled by such memories but at this place in my journey, I've learned to cope with my ghosts.

I'm not much to look at anymore but in my time, I was a frisky dog! I want to tell you, I was top notch in a fight or at least I believed so, not ever having been in one with another dog. Remember what I said earlier about the raised eye? Understand that preceding any fight one needs to have a *no-backing-down* approach, prior to the physical confrontation. The lip is lifted in various degrees to expose the right number of teeth and gum. The back and neck hair rise, along with a deep throaty growl that reaches down to the inner depths of a dog's spirit. Then there is the eye with its detached look that says to the observer, "*This creature is possessed by dark forces, but not really.*" After all the center stage theatrics are over, one needs to be totally aggressive and go for the throat, an eye, or any soft area that will cause extreme pain. Finally, know when you're beaten and run like the wind.

Without sounding like I'm howling at the moon, or risk using human clichés, I guess you could say that I was dog's dog. But those days are over as well as the days of fighting for turf and honor. Today I've come accustomed to a warm bed in a safe place. I ended up with a good boss, in fact several over the years, who treated me well. As I lay here, I find it only fitting to tell my story and where a life with no leash took me.

The wind blew gently against the bedroom curtains as I dreamed away the afternoon. I was the last of the litter remaining and, being so, was able to stay for just better than a year's time after my brothers and sister had been given away. My mom had had her last litter of pups and now was content to age gracefully in the company of this family.

In my dream, I was somewhere wandering the backyard and my nose was sniffing a butterfly on a Zinnia. Beneath the leaves of a Hosta, I spied a toad and followed closely behind him as he tried to find a corner where he might hide. I stayed on him until a bumblebee took me in another direction. Part of my dream was based on reality, while some was acquired from the visual box in what the family called *the living room* where the device was kept.

Having had enough of my blissful dream, the fates would make the next move. The wind gave an extra push on the bedroom door and bang! So much for my serenity. The door found itself in the closed position, while I was raised to a half-sitting, half ready to defend my territory stance. My eyes were wide open, but my brain was still trying to kick in. After a long second or two, I realized what had happened and stretched my torso out, to loosen my muscles and shake the sleep from my head.

Oh well, I thought to myself, *time to relieve the bladder.*

I bounded off my caretaker's bed and sat at the base of the door where I whimpered lightly. The female was around and would eventually hear me. Her approach was much softer and pleasant, as is with the reproductive humans. The male was quiet but kind. He would say more with a rub behind the ears, showing his genuine affection, rather than with a lot of needless dialogue that never amounted to much anyway. The talkers were always looking for an answer that they themselves would insert in their speech. If we dogs were verbally given a chance to respond to their jabber, they might not like what they heard.

The true measure of a man human was how he handled a situation in which another of my species or I had created. Some act that was less than appealing to the way of life of these characters. Relieving oneself on the floor somewhere in the master's house always brought a response. Mostly a vocal response but sometimes physical. I learned to dodge the thing called the newspaper. However, there were ways to get out of the pain, which was quickly learned. The shameful look was used by slinking out of the room with the head lowered, but the eyes still making contact. Moving slowly in the direction of the closest escape route with one's tail between the legs and the ears dragging on the floor would get you either enough sympathy at the time or enough distance to avoid the rolled-up evening news. Sadly enough, at the first experience with this in the post puppy stage, a dog thinks it is all right and wears a happy face after the fact because the dog is relieved! That look is eradicated quickly.

Now, if the female is the one to find the mess, then the dialogue goes something like . . . "Oh, look what you've done! Did you take the dog out dear? *We* need to clean this up!"

There are so many lessons to learn at the beginning. They just don't understand that because we dogs do not do things their way, it does not necessarily make it wrong. Think for a moment, that if you were to examine something, would you not pick it up to feel its texture, its weight, and its makeup? That is why a human has hands. Well, a dog can't always do things that way, so we stick our noses in it to see if it has a favorable aroma. We might push with the snout to roll a thing over or scratch with the paw on occasion, but ultimately the smell is what attracts or repels us. If an object is undesirable, we, many times, will mark it so another of our species is not caught unprepared. This will also notify the examinee that this particular thing or place has been looked over and has a temporary claim to the geography at hand. I'm getting a little away from my story though and will try to bring things back to those days after I reached some maturity.

After some patience on my part and the steady high-pitched, almost heartbreaking whine, the female heard the call. The door was opened to my relief. A few minutes more and I would have had to bark out loud! I went into the happy face, with my tongue hanging loosely as I headed for the backdoor. I passed my mom on the way through the living room where she occupied her favorite corner. Tail wagging and that impatient dance of the four paws got a favorable response, to which the backdoor was opened.

"Good dog! Go do your job now," the female called out, as if I needed guidance at this time. The next part is a bit personal but when a human goes into a bathroom, I would suspect that the toilet seat is checked out and then mounted. There would even be additional movement just to position everything in the right place. I ask you then, why is it so remarkably funny when we dogs look for our exact spot of deposit?

Part of making it all work is the sticky paw dance. By that I mean, we dogs get into the physical position by arching our back as we step around in what appears to be a circle. Our paws give off the impression that we have just stepped into puddle of molasses and are lifting each paw in an attempt at separation. Could you do all of this while some other species is watching you? The goofy young boy from the next dwelling would sometimes stand in his yard pointing at me, while laughing out loud to others or himself. I thought he was touched. How embarrassing! I could do nothing but continue because once you start, that's all you can do until you're finished. No matter, I guess.

Life changed quickly that day in the yard. I could hear the female returning inside to stop the ringing thing she called her cellphone. She would talk to it to get it to stop the ringing, I believe. As I finished my routine and began to explore the confines of the yard, I realized that the gate had been left open. The explorer in me never hesitated, as I moved gingerly through the opening realizing a whole new world stretched out before me. I never looked back. I never heard her call my name. As I think in retrospect upon that time in my life, I wasn't happy with my given name anyway. Roscoe sounded more like a name for a monkey than a dog. I had seen one on the box they called a television some time ago. So, shedding the uncomfortable handle I was given, two square meals a day, a warm corner to curl up in, and a short life of security in the suburbs, I headed into the unknown. At this place in time, I figured on returning but happenings tend to lead us in other directions.

Many things passed by my eyes. Some of the visuals registered while others simply were filed away in my mind for future reference. There were colors, sounds, birds, and cars speeding quickly by. In addition, there were children playing on the lawns, then a squirrel scampered up a tree trunk as it shook its tail as a warning. All these things filled my senses. Such a flood of sensations poured over me as I moved across this unfamiliar terrain. I stopped in my tracks as I spotted my first cat. I knew I wanted to bite it, but I didn't know why. There was something old, within my ancient blood stream, that boiled when I laid eyes upon that slinky, furry thing with those piercing eyes. It crouched and peered in my direction with the hair on its back rising toward the sky. Hissing at me only increased my loathing and my lip began to rise over my canines as a deep throaty growl passed out of my mouth from the depths of my inner place.

As I was about to make chase, an iridescent green dragonfly with large red eyes landed on my nose. Wings extending beyond either side of my nose made me look as if I had a bow tied on the end of my snout. The encounter was brief but startling for both parties and we immediately made for opposite ends of the universe. Composure returned but by that time, the cat had made its way to obscurity, while I was left to file yet, another experience temporarily away until a later date.

Many sounds filled my ears. These too would be filed then sorted through over time. There were good sounds such as children's laughter and the songs of the birds. There were frightful sounds, like that of a fire engine passing or the screeching of a car's tires. Then there were sounds, which currently were not identifiable. The drone of an unseen airplane, a factory whistle, and many other noises passed through my tender ears.

As I crossed the street, I continued on my way heading into the midday sun. I looked to my right and saw the neighbor boy, as I disappeared into the field across the road. Entering it on one end and exiting on another end, I cut through a couple of backyards and eventually found my way down along the railroad crossing. A rabbit caught my eye, and I chased it along the length of track for some time. Breaking into the underbrush I followed the fuzzy creature, losing it in a matter of minutes. At the time, I was not aware that they would slip down a hole in the ground.

Somewhere in the passing hours, my old town faded behind me as I traversed field after field. The fields were bordered by an occasional road made of asphalt or dirt. The world was a much larger place than I had imagined. As time moved my life forward, I would come to understand that there was more out here than I would have cared to have in my bowl. Some things were buried like a forgotten bone. Various places and encounters could have been erased from my days but as it is, we must accept the bad as well as the good. It is what defines us.

Not knowing this made my existence seem strained at times and I wondered why this or that had happened to me. The makeup of the world I shared with so many other creatures seemed to me, to be pieces of a puzzle intricately mixed together like a fine soup, which only needed to simmer for a while. The whole being better than the parts.

The sun was beginning to set as I made my way. I had no idea where I was going nor did I care, because I found myself to be in awe of all I saw, smelled, and tasted. The sounds alerted me to both joy and danger. I was not yet baptized in danger and still believed that the world was a fun-loving place. Without realizing my path, I had come to venture on almost a parallel route with that of the railroad tracks. After an hour of moving about in the dark, I felt I needed to find a place to bed down for the night. I was drawn to the glow of a small campfire and as I approached, I realized that it was tucked under the bridge that the metal rails ran over. There was a dry creek beneath the trestle.

I remained just outside of the halo of the fire, as not to be detected until I had assessed the situation that played out before me. A simple tune played softly over the summer air, as one of the two figures forced his breath back and forth through the openings in a harmonica. Marrying several notes together placed a harmonious flow on the air, which perked my ears in pleasure.

Something was cooking over the fire and the scent of food had my attention as well. I dared to venture forward and broke the barrier between darkness and light. Making myself visible, I stopped to get a read from the two men.

"Hey! Whatcha want dog?" the first man said.

From my brief knowledge of people, he looked to be in his early thirties. That assessment was in human years. His skin was pale with tired red eyes. A tan baseball cap that had seen better days was perched high on his head. It had a truck emblem on the front. His bomber jacket had small rips in the sleeves and much of the leather's surface had a sanded appearance. The jacket had seen a lifetime on somebody's back. A black tee shirt, jeans, and work boots finished the portrait. He smelled of something, which made me wary.

"He's hungry, is all," the second man added, as he rested the hand holding the harmonica on his knee.

The second man, who was older by fifteen years or so, gently tapped his other hand against the side of his khaki pants, as to call me over to his side. I slinked gradually toward him with my head low but my eyes open to both men. Each step was measured as I gained entrance to the circle. Letting the music man touch my head, then scratch me gently behind the ears gave way to a small measure of trust. Appearances, as they were, gave me more confidence in the music man. He was much neater in the way he wore his dark green jacket and fedora. His clothing was not new by any means but looked well kept. Even his boots were clean compared to the other man's.

"Are you hungry dog? Is that what it is?" the first man asked as he rubbed the stubble on his chin and neck.

He pulled a few scraps of bread out of a bag and tossed them my way. The older man gave me the remains of a can of hash. I ate the bread then worked the can with my tongue to get every bit out of the container. The music man gave way with an agreeable smile as I was given my first handout. When I finished, I moved quickly to the edge of the lighted area, where I positioned myself in the prone, eyes towards the fire. It wasn't much of a meal, but it took away the emptiness. The older man took the empty tin and filled it with water he had in a plastic jug. He placed it about three feet from me then returned to his spot. I got back up, sniffed it then lapped it up with my tongue. When I emptied it, the older man filled it again. I took another drink then returned to my previous spot.

Afterward, I was blessed with a couple of melodies from the musician, as he soulfully played to the first quarter moon in the night sky. The younger man stared off toward nowhere while the other played. He kept reaching into his jacket pocket to retrieve a small bottle, unscrewed the cap, and drank some of its contents. Although I was tired, my eyes never left either man until they themselves decided to bed down for the night. I had a gut feeling that the older man, who had a seasoned look about him, was indeed trustable. The other one made a dog shiver. He had a vacant look about him. I felt him to be a troubled soul even though at this stage in my life, I knew not what that meant. His appearance was that of a treacherous flight down a long hill of briars, stumps, and holes. There was nothing that told of a good day with this one.

I relocated to a place close to the fire but kept it between my hosts and myself. Exhausted, I drifted away to a warm memory. A couple of hours before daybreak arrived, I was dreaming there was a struggle between the two men. The lid lifted on my right eye at the sound of a thud, and I immediately felt there was movement, as a dark figure approached me. Jumping up on all fours, I dodged the knife that he tried to imbed in my back. The blade glistened briefly in the air and his second swing of the arm caught me across the snout. I yelped, running into the brush behind me. This feeling was something new, something dark, that made my being fill with something I would learn later in life called fear.

Moving through the brush like the wind, I could hear his footsteps fade. I made progress through the early morning darkness, trying to avoid running into the small scrub trees that dotted the field. I eventually made my way into a low area that ran along the woods. I could tell that water accumulated here in early spring but for now it was dry, as dry as the creek bed. As the black of night began to gray into dawn, I slipped past the first trees and disappeared into the small wood line. My snout was bleeding and it hurt. I needed to lie down and lower my heart rate. Finding an area where I could make a quick retreat with two escape routes to choose from, I crawled into some taller grass at the edge of a small opening in the trees.

Falling into a half sleep, I rested for about ninety minutes listening to the dark silence turn to the morning song of many birds. This was a gentle awakening. Reluctantly, I made my way to an erect position. I looked back through the trees toward the direction of the field I had crossed in great haste and hoped the bad man had given up on me. My snout had begun to scab, and the bleeding had temporarily ceased, but I still needed to take great care not to bump it for it was a deep cut.

Now, as it is with us dogs, we are likely to just move on with our lives, usually because we are distracted by the next thing that happens. I was hungry again. Realizing where my last meal came from, I made my way slowly through the early morning mist that hung just above the fields of scrub trees, brush, and grass. I moved back in the direction of last night's offering. Cautiously, I came closer to the area where the two men were camped the night before. I could see the railroad bridge but decided to alter my approach from the previous night and move in from a different angle. My stomach outweighed my sense of safety as I crossed the tracks further away from the bridge and moved to the opposite side. Looking down towards where the two men had greeted me, there was zero movement, nor did I hear anything. I moved down the slope to below the railroad bridge. Where there once was a warm fire, only a few smoldering ashes remained. Slumped over on one side was the music man who still appeared to be asleep. The other odd character was nowhere to be seen.

Moving forward at a cautious pace, I worked my way around to where I had eaten last night's meal. Sniffing the ground, the can, and eventually the surrounding area, I came up empty. Curiosity drew me toward the music man who had not moved a muscle. I sniffed the empty bottle the knife man had been drinking from and a few discarded sandwich bags, looking for leftovers. Nose first, I sniffed his shoe, working my way up his pants leg to where his shirt was dark and red. I moved my nose toward the puddle of blood and stepped back a bit, looking quickly around. There was no sign of anyone. My gut instinct was to leave the area. This man was void of life. Not entirely familiar with something like this, I stammered around and whimpered a little. There was a sadness that befell me, and I knew I would miss this man because of his gentle nature. I had enjoyed the music that he played. Fear pushed me along, as I did not want to be discovered by the strange man. I looked to my rear one last time as I moved up the length of track that faded toward the north.

Two days of roaming the countryside netted me no more than increased hunger. There were a few wildflowers I found worthy of consumption and enjoyed, until I got stung by a bee right on the forehead! I kept close to the tracks using them as a reference, as I made my way past an old house trailer no longer lived in. The windows were all knocked out and one end appeared to have had a small fire awhile back. The charred walls stunk so I kept moving on. I thought I smelled the strange man's drink, but it was hard to tell with the scent of burnt plastic and wood still in my nostrils.

Further down the tracks there were a few tires, bottles, cans, and an assortment of odd junk one would encounter in a rural area where the weeds tried to hide the garbage. An occasional road intersected the tracks and although I was tempted to try one or two of them, I remained steadfast to my route.

On the third morning, I awoke to the sound of a truck blowing its horn off in the distance. I stood and stretched, letting out a little squeak as I yawned. The top of my snout smarted from the cut as well as the bee sting on my head. The wound started bleeding the previous day but had stopped again during the night. It throbbed constantly in this early stage of healing. The tall grass made for a nice bed, but I was beginning to tire of sleeping under the stars. My empty stomach once again reminded me that I needed food. I grabbed a drink from a small pool of stagnant water and took a quick look at myself in the reflection. I looked like a lost idea. Funny, I never thought once of returning to the family I was born into, even after my misfortunes.

Back on the tracks, I crossed one more road and things began to change. It looked like civilization had found a place to camp. This was an old industrial area that I was walking into. Several railroad spurs split off to some dead-end tracks that held many boxcars. Parts of train equipment were scattered over several acres of land. An impression of something that once was alive and then like the harmonica man, void of life, seemed to be a good way of describing this place. A train engine idled on the other side of the railroad yard.

I followed a spur toward the buildings. There were a few factories near the end of the town and as I moved forward there were signs of people. I started to notice a few men working around the loading docks near the tracks. One of the men was sitting on the dock eating and offered me half of his sandwich. "That's a nasty cut you have there pooch," he exclaimed. He wanted to pet me, but I was afraid even after he fed me. After I ate, I moved on. Vehicles moved everywhere, along with other new noises from all different sources breaking the silence of the countryside. Soon there were intersecting streets which began to appear at regular intervals.

I bid farewell to the occasional rabbit or red-winged blackbird and looked for some place where a dog might get some more nourishment. I turned a hard right and walked up the side of a hill to a city street. There was some traffic as I approached. That made me wary. A few businesses filled the next block or two with spaces in between like old men's teeth. Several machine shops, metal fabricating shops, and warehouses were open for business. This was a very old part of town with a few houses and empty lots sporadically dropped in and around some of the shops. When I crossed the street and began my way down the third city block, I heard voices inside a concrete block building. It had an old sliding door on a rusty rail which was slid back in the open position. A tarred roof slanted from the front side to back gave the rain a path to follow. I could see smoke spewing from the pipe, which extended through the roof toward the sky.

"Paper is going for sixty-eight cents a hundred pounds," one old timer told a younger man in his early twenties, as he helped unload the trunk of his car. He stacked the bundles of old newspapers on a scale which was set in the concrete floor. Slowly, he chomped on the second half of a fat smoldering cigar waiting for the scale to settle.

"Three hundred and forty pounds. Let's see . . . that'll get you two dollars and thirty-one cents."

The younger guy looked dejected but took the money, closed his trunk, and drove away without a word. I walked in front of the open door and caught the old man's eye.

"Hey there, fella! That's a nasty cut you have there."

Moving slowly towards the outstretched hand I lowered my head and let the wrinkled fingers rub my ears. He seemed OK, although I was a bit shy from my previous experience with humans.

"Let's see if I got something in the fridge you could eat. You look like it's been a while since you had a good meal."

The old man rummaged around for a minute or two and came out with a container of leftover pork roast with carrots and potatoes.

"This is a few days old, but I don't think you'll mind," he said, as he put the container on the floor minus the lid. He returned to a desk and chair where he conducted business from. The phone rang and the cigar was briefly deposited in a dark blue ashtray.

"University Salvage! How can I help you?"

I moved right in and devoured the meal all the while keeping one eye on the geezer. After the call, he fiddled with a worn-out radio that had half an antenna with a coat hanger completing the final extension. Finally, he got a station of oldies music dialed in or at least that's what he mumbled they were called. The songs were upbeat and added a pleasant touch to the atmosphere.

As a courtesy, when I was finished, I walked over and shoved my head under his hand. He hummed to the music, looked down and said, "That's a good boy."

"Bet you could use some water too!" He got an old ceramic bowl, rinsed it out and filled it with cold water. I lapped half a bowl down, found a corner with an old throw rug on the floor and curled up for a nap. I felt secure for the first time in a while. Belly full, I drifted off to sleep.

A kid pulled up to the door with a load of magazines and newspapers in his coaster wagon. About that time, I sat up, yawned, then stretched, and returned to the water bowl. The old man told the boy that the magazines were seventy-five cents a hundred pound, and the newspaper was sixty-eight cents a hundred. The boy put the magazines on the scale, and it registered fifty-five pounds, then he put the newspaper on the scale and that weighed seventy-nine pounds. He netted himself ninety-five cents and was down the sidewalk in a methodical pull, the wagon rattling over the separations in the concrete.

I walked out the open door and looked at the lad shrink in the distance.

"Are you ready to move on dog?" The old man queried scratching his balding head.

I thought a bit and looked back into the building.

"You're welcome to stay if you like. My old mascot went to dog heaven a few months ago. It'd be nice to have the company."

I walked over to the stop sign near the corner, lifted my leg, then returned to the rug which ended up being my bed for the next couple of years. Being the junkyard dog was a bit of prestige for me. It felt like a merit badge in my life. I kept the old man company, plus I would growl low when someone gave him a hard time on a price for something, whether they were selling or buying. After a few years, I was known to the regulars as the accountant.

When there were no customers, the boss would spend a lot of time out in the junkyard burning the plastic coating off the wire he'd retrieve from old electrical motors and other sources. I always stayed up wind for it burned my nose and eyes when I got a face full.

The junkyard was divided into several areas out back of the scale and office area. There were old cars and parts on one acre. Another section had worn out appliances from refrigerators to stoves, dishwashers, etc. All doors were removed as a safety precaution. Another area contained a variety of pipe from one-half inch to culvert size. There were old sinks and bathtubs mostly without the hardware. The hardware was piled up in wooden crates near the porcelain. Different metals were separated in piles around the yard. There was a semitrailer for the paper and another for cardboard. A distinctive smell rose from the place, which covered about three and a half acres in all.

The office hadn't been cleaned since Moses was a boy, but I didn't care. There was a potbellied woodstove to keep the chill out in winter. My rug was near the stove. The stove also served as a place for a few regulars to congregate and shoot the breeze. The boss would get a pickup truck load of wood every so often. A few of the regulars chipped in for the heat. The refrigerator was painted a pea green and made noises like it was possessed but there was always something in there to eat. There was another sliding metal door which opened to the junkyard out back and one window on that side of the shack, which was so dirty, I hadn't noticed it the first couple of months I was boarding.

One late morning as I was sunning myself, I spotted my natural enemy out of the corner of my eye. I waited quietly as if I were asleep, in hopes that the furry nemesis would pass within reach. She was an ugly cat of gray with a bit of dirty brown running through her coat. There was haughtiness in her demeanor, like she owned the place. Although the boss seldom fed her, she managed to live nicely off the mice and birds who forgot she was around. Many times, she would disappear for a couple of days but always returned to the junkyard. There were many places to hide in and around the cars. With all the other junk, it must have appeared to be a resort to her. Occasionally, she'd hook up with a Tom and they'd fill the night air with odd noises and hissing.

I'd been trying to sink my teeth into that arrogant pain for some time but all it ever got me was a swipe across the nose with her paw. None the less, I continued my pursuit as would any decent dog with a vendetta.

On a late afternoon while I was in the middle of my siesta, I heard a voice which chilled my bones and brought me to my feet. I had been a resident for just over two years in man's time. My boss was talking to a guy about the price of brass when I went ballistic, charging at the man. I stopped short remembering the knife but raised my fur, curled my lip, and snapped my jaws, emitting a sound which said, *death awaits you stranger.*

"Looks like your dog needs to be taught some manners old man," the drifter challenged.

"I think he's got rabies," the old man countered. This made the drifter back off toward the door.

I remembered the scoundrel too well and I'm sure he recognized his handiwork on my snout. The old man had affectionately named me scar face, aka the accountant, which worked at the time for me.

"Well, I'll come back some other time when things are quieter," the drifter said.

The drifter's eyes met mine and he knew that I knew what he was all about. Chances are his intentions were to cause harm to the boss. I didn't want to see my provider quiet like the harmonica man. As he walked across the street, moving down the block, I followed out to the sidewalk barking my fool head off. I didn't want him around the potbellied stove or near the place.

After the incident the boss bent down to pat my side as I huffed and puffed a bit while I tried to calm down.

"You recognized that bad penny, didn't you boy?! Don't you worry. I got a gun in the desk for just such varmints."

We never saw him again.

CHAPTER 2

One midmorning moving quietly along the path between the appliances and the section of pipes and culverts, the annoying feline stopped short of the open area of the yard. Her front right paw hesitated like she was testing the water before jumping in. I watched from the shadows and could take no more! I sprung to my feet with a low throated growl and sped to the spot which she occupied only a second before. That cat bounced straight up and landed on a large culvert section, then a jump over a dryer, and between two old stoves. After that, it was all me barking my head off, knowing I had failed again.

The time will come, I thought, *when I would get my due.* And yet, I really didn't have an issue with her other than she was a cat.

Seasons passed and the pursuit continued. It was as if that feline tempted me out of pure boredom. It was two winters later when I failed for the last time at an attempt to clamp my jaws on that fur ball's hindquarter. Unfortunately, it was a terrible day for me.

It was early January, so there had been many snowstorms by this time. In between, there were a few sunny days where some of the snow melted, creating icy spots where the water pooled in the junkyard. I'd lay low, usually not too far from the woodstove near the scale, where the old man weighed and paid for the materials brought in. The safe and cashbox was in a closet, but the boss never locked the door. I think he felt, I was his alarm if anything foul happened.

One afternoon I had taken a short walk outside to relieve my bladder on an old pickup the boss was currently driving. On returning inside I went out back in the junkyard. I started down the aisle of stacked car shells, where I ran right into that demonized cat.

"Hsss" was all I heard as I bolted toward that dark spirit. We both maneuvered between the cars and parts scattered throughout the yard. The cat was in the lead with me snapping my jaws close behind. If not for the seriousness of the chase, I'd have laughed at the cartoon scene come to life. I was right on top of her when I hit a long icy patch. I lost my footing and slid about five feet crashing into the side of an old milk delivery truck that was missing its front wheels. At the time, I wasn't aware that the access door had been removed from its hinges and was only set in position. Adding to its weight was a good amount of ice inside the door. It accumulated from the constant thaw and freeze off the truck's roof throughout the day. My impact caused the door to fall straight down, severing part of my left front leg, three or so inches above the paw. The ground was rock hard and with gravity as it is, it sliced the appendage off like a guillotine. Pain overwhelmed me!

My yelping brought the old man running to my aid. He brought me and the appendage inside and covered the leg with some clean rags. The boss called the veterinarian, locked up the shop and got me on the front seat of his pickup truck. I was indebted to my boss for getting me to the vet, where I was put under. That placed me in temporary peace. It was a three days later when I regained consciousness, returning to reality. The vet kept me sedated so I wouldn't be moving around. I didn't realize at first the seriousness of my injury until a couple of weeks passed by and I tried to stand erect. When the front leg is injured severally enough, they remove the leg up to the body cavity. I was hospitalized for a several weeks. Through the next couple of months, I was given special treatment by the old man. He made sure I was eating and drinking. I didn't catch on that he was hiding an antibiotic and something to help me sleep within the liver sausage he was giving me daily as a treat. After a month at the junkyard, my caretaker took me for a return visit to the vet, where I heard by the tone of their voices that the surgery was healing well. It had been six weeks; however, I was still in some pain. I wanted to pull the bandages from my torso and give it a lick or two.

Over time, I overcame my handicap and learned to sort of hop about. It was strange to me that everything I had lifted my leg to pee on were now part of my support system to lean upon, so I wouldn't fall over when I raised my rear leg. Kids who accompanied their parents to the junkyard often tried to get close to see the three-legged dog. With most of those kids, I let out a low growl. Still, every once in a while, I thought that I needed some affection, as did they, so I'd let down my guard as long as they didn't try to touch my scar.

That thorn of a cat got hers. One morning in early spring, about four months after my accident, I took a walk out front to the hydrant. To my great surprise laid a flattened version of my nemesis. I moved slowly toward the carcass looking in both directions, so I too, didn't end up a spot on the street. I thought of lifting my leg on her, but she was an admirable adversary. I couldn't find it in my person to blame her for my lost appendage. That was my own doing.

Another year passed by before the old man died. He treated me well and I was very fond of him. The boss's daughter fed me for a few weeks after her father was gone. It was a nice gesture. The junkyard was outdated and eventually was razed in lieu of an apartment complex. When the big machinery came in to clear the junk and the land, it was time for me to move on. I headed north of all directions, but it was summer and there were great smells in the air. I was going on seven in human years by this time.

From my earlier encounters I found that the railroad tracks were the highway of adventure, so I moved out of town the same way I entered. There was less of a chance to be messed with in my handicapped state if I traveled the rails.

When I got to the outskirts of the next town, I befriended a guy who road in the caboose of a passing freight train that pulled into this new rail-yard. This tall, thin individual in his late forties, sported a set of bib overalls, gray long-sleeved undershirt, and a striped engineer's hat. He was in the yard for a few days waiting for the boxcars to be organized. Once finished,

1 CALL ME BLESSED

the train would move north and south with various materials for delivery. I did my best to suck up for a meal and I could tell he was talking to me by the nickname he bestowed upon me.

"Hey, Shorty! Want the rest of this soup?"

I thought, *Shorty? That's not a name for a dog! I wonder if it's in reference to my stump?*

He tossed in the end piece of a loaf of bread as well. I took it and began a partnership of sorts. He'd feed me and I'd let him scratch my ears. When it was time for the train to pull out, he asked if I'd like to come aboard. I whimpered a bit and looked pitifully at the caboose's stairs, so he picked me up and brought me into his house on wheels.

The twin diesel engines pulled steady as the string of boxcars were jerked into submission. Finally, the caboose got the end jolt, which made me jump slightly at the tremors. Large steel wheels moved across the length of track slowly at first, then accelerating as the engines took command of the railroad car chain, linked together by couplers. The whole scene was powerful!

Coffee filled the air in this cabin on wheels. There were four stopovers in a two-day period. Boxcars were deposited in each rail yard as well as various tanker cars, which carried everything from acids to petroleum products. New additions were moved into position and added to the train for the return trip.

Over the next month I made myself welcome. The sandy haired railroad man would pluck a small banjo he kept in the corner near his bunk. I wouldn't say he was very good, but I did find a certain comfort in the gesture he made by trying. His singing was much like the sounds that surround old boxcars aged with rust. It was a creaking sort of sound, which on one occasion got me to howl. I believe he took offense to my joining in, by believing I was ridiculing his vocal abilities. That, however, was not the case. I just felt compelled to join in. Regardless, I laid back down as I got the look of annoyance tossed my way, returning to my place as the observer.

On one evening, he made a comment that I smelled like a dead horse. I suppose he had a valid point but as I went through my card catalog of smells, I could not remember a dead horse. After a certain amount of coaxing, he talked me into a bath. There was a large metal tub he filled with warm water and soap. After the ordeal was over, I noticed that the fleas had momentarily jumped ship. That was a sweet relief although it didn't last long.

One day led to another and before I knew it, I had stayed put for three months moving up and down on the rails. Even though I knew I was giving up a belly full of warm meals I opted to move along. I whimpered that morning, which was my way of saying I needed to go relieve myself. He answered my call and carried me down the caboose's metal grated steps. I moved down the crest of the track bed, looked back at the empty doorway then moved into the brush. I thought I heard him call out "Shorty" but I was a fair distance away and could have been mistaken. He was a good sort, treating me like family but no matter, for my mind was focused ahead. I was on the outskirts of some major town. I could tell by the size of the railroad yard. I separated myself from the tracks and followed a path along the interstate for the better part of the day, eventually poking around some trash cans behind a service station.

Some cantankerous attendant drove me away with some harsh words and by tossing a few stones in my direction. When one bounced off the pavement and struck me in the guts I hopped away into the tall grass across the road. I didn't understand his actions. I had learned when living at the junkyard that there are all kinds of people. There were those people that dropped in where the scale was seated at the junkyard. Some to sell and others just to talk like they did. Anyway, I learned that although there were millions of personalities, all fell into two categories. That was either good or bad.

Following the asphalt on a side road took me away from the interstate and the tracks. I took to the edge of the road, remembering the flat cat and made my way into the countryside. It just happened to be my luck to stumble upon some baby raccoons. I remember hearing a hissing sound but unlike a cat. The next thing I knew, I was being attacked by what I can best describe as a crazy mother type. I ran or hobbled the best I could in the opposite direction but not before being bit in the back as well as scratched numerous times about the head, neck, and ears. Distance was my best defense.

After what seemed like a few miles of hopping I sat down for a rest at the edge of a small wayside that bordered a flowing creek. I got a drink from the creek. There was a scattering of picnic tables under the cover of crab apple and pine trees. Here, I felt, I had gained sufficient distance between the raccoon and her family. She had her brood to attend to, so I was the least of her concerns. Exhaustion overcame me and I fell into a deep sleep. I tossed a few memories around in my head as I slept, grunting, and squeaking out little sounds as I dreamt. The rumble of a car pulling on to the gravel woke me to my feet. A small, older woman opened the car door and headed toward the plain beige building which housed restrooms.

On her return to the car, she noticed me at the edge of the grass. She had a sweet voice, as she cooed a greeting in my direction. I stretched and let out a little whine to show I was a peaceable sort and that it was OK to approach me. This began a wonderful relationship, which lasted a couple of years.

"You poor thing," she said. "What happened to your leg? And all those scars, oh my! You look like you've been in a, uh, dog, you know, fight. Maybe several fights!

"Are you lost? Orphaned? How'd you like to come home with me?"

I gave it some thought as I looked her over. She wore white sneakers, jeans, and a light green windbreaker over a pale yellow tee shirt. Her silver hair was tied back in a bun and as she talked to me, she peered over her glasses. My stomach spoke up and I agreed within that I was hungry. I answered by wagging my tail, while I still had one and as an affirmation, I let her scratch my back and the underside of my neck.

Ahhh! That felt good!

I thought I caught the faint scent of beef on her hands as I sniffed her. She opened the passenger door on her silver vehicle, and I made my way up without any help to the floor, then perched myself on the front seat. She got in on the other side joining me. Starting the car, she put it in drive and moved down the road.

"You'll need a bath," she cooed, as we made our way.

Yeah! Drown those fleas, I thought.

When we arrived at her house near the edge of town, I was awarded some leftover chicken she deboned. Later, after my belly was full, I found a nice place on the front porch to take a siesta. While I napped, the old woman left in her car. She came back a short time later and carried some groceries into the house. On her second trip to the car, she returned with two medium bags of dog food. She promptly filled a bowl. The smell of the nuggets in the bowl got my tail wagging again. Memories of a domestic setting made me feel good, for it seemed I had found a home one more time. A real home with a backyard but no fence.

After a few weeks of various children showing up, and a few adults, I came to realize that my keeper was a piano teacher by trade. I enjoyed the woman's playing; however, the kids were hard on the ears. I would find a place at the far end of the porch until they were done. The lessons always took one revolution of the clock. At the end there were words exchanged regarding practice then the old woman would say, "See you next week."

Most everyone who came for a lesson was a good soul and was kind to me, but there is always a bitter peanut in the bag.

His name was Terrance. The first time he came to the old woman's house I felt a chill go through my body. This young boy of eleven had more than a conniving nature. He dripped of evil, and I thought, *This could be the man with the knife as a child.* His mother would drop him off at the mailbox near the road and you could feel that he wanted nothing to do with piano lessons as he walked reluctantly to the house. His eyes were dark and he always seemed to be scanning the area to see what mischief he could light the fuse on. His cunning ways were only out shone by his angelic innocence when confronted.

When our eyes met briefly, I felt unnerved. He caught a glimpse of me as I slipped around the corner of the house, moving toward the backyard. To my surprise, he followed after me.

"Damn! A three-legged dog," he said under his breath.

The old woman must have observed him through the window because she came out on the porch and called to him.

"Terrence, it's time for your lesson."

Reluctantly, he made his way back to the front door and disappeared from my sight. I always knew when Terrence was coming for his piano lesson. I could hear his mother's car when it approached the house. The car was in bad shape mechanically. That was my cue to leave the porch, making myself invisible. He still would try and sneak around the property looking for me. I bothered him for some reason. There was a saccharine touch in his voice that wasn't quite normal as he called out, "Dog! Where are you dog?" Staying under the garden shed in the shadows was the best medicine for me.

Months passed as I became a fixture around the place. The old woman treated me very well. Many times, after dinner, I'd spend the evenings watching the television with her. I'd let out an occasional bark when I heard movement outside. It gave me purpose and I hoped it gave my boss a feeling of security. During the day I made my way around the property exploring the garden and some apple trees that were behind the shed. Beyond the apple trees there was several wooded acres at the back of the property. Beyond the boss's property, the forest rambled on. I would venture into the woods a few feet, but it was difficult to maneuver through the brush with my handicap. Eventually, I would return to the porch and nap in the sun.

The summer passed by as did autumn. Winter was a drastic change in my daily routine. It was difficult for me to maneuver in the snow, so most days I'd wait until someone came by to clear the way or I'd do my duty near the base of the steps. It bothered the old woman, but I could see in her eyes that she understood. I stayed in the front hall during the day when piano lessons were being taught. The cold got to me, making me ache, and I appreciated the heat blowing out from the floor vent. Timing my bathroom breaks, I'd let out a high-pitched yawn to let the old woman know it was time for her to open the door and let me relieve myself. A small picket fence was where I would lean to urinate. I guess you might say there was a balance and an understanding between my caretaker and me.

I believe the seasons had passed by at least twice and then some, when in late spring I was taken by surprise. As I said before, I knew the sound of the mother's car, which delivered Terrence to the front gate. What I was not prepared for was the mother getting a different car.

I was sound asleep on the porch when I was startled by the boy's presence. I quickly got to my remaining feet and hobbled down the length of the wrap around porch to the side set of stairs.

"What's the matter freak? Don't you like me?" The boy remarked, as he followed me down the stairs. I kept moving toward the shed as he picked up a rock. When I turned to look back at him the rock hit me right in the eye. I yelped loudly, which brought the old woman out of the back door of the house and to my aid. Bleeding profusely, I continued to howl in pain.

"What have you done Terrence?!" the old woman screamed.

"Nothing! The dog snapped at me! Honest!" he said, although it somehow was not convincing enough for Ruth, the piano teacher.

"You're an evil sort. I'm calling your mother. I'm finished with you. Go sit on the front steps until she comes to pick you up," the teacher said, as she tended to me. And forty minutes later I was introduced to another veterinarian.

That was the last I ever saw of Terrence and the last I ever saw out of that eye. It wasn't necessary to remove the eye, but I was unable to see out of it anymore after it healed.

Right eye, left lower leg, knife cut across the snout, chewed ears all came to mind. *What could possibly be next?*

The vet that took care of my injury commented that I was running out of parts and maybe I should be put down. I didn't like the sound of that nor did the old woman, as I could see by the frown on her face. On our last visit, she thanked him for services rendered and closed the conversation with a goodbye.

"Never you mind about that," she said firmly to me. She packed me up and got me on the front seat of her car. I looked forward to returning to her home where I rested for weeks in front of the sofa as I healed. After a month of salve and bandages, I was back to a kind of normal.

She was very attentive to me, changing my dressing daily and making sure I was well fed. I remembered the medicine trick the junkyard boss had done with me when I lost the leg but there was no liver sausage this time. A soft cheese made for a grand substitute.

The beginning of autumn brought about another change in my life. My dear friend and companion ceased to move one late evening. I found her on the floor of the kitchen. This was much like the harmonica man and my junkyard boss but different in a sense. Her teacup was shattered, and the liquid was splattered across the linoleum. It was as if she left her body in a hurry. I whimpered for a time and thought, *Why does this happen to me?*

It was midmorning the next day, before someone came to the door for a lesson. I barked my fool head off and finally they came in finding the piano teacher on the floor. I knew that there was a drastic change that had taken place. Making my way down the porch, I moved past the front yard while the commotion went from shock to the student mother's telephone call to 911. I heard the piano student crying as I turned to look back briefly, beginning the next leg of my journey. No pun intended. Wandering for a few weeks brought me to a vision of many lights on the horizon one night.

I was exhausted but knew I needed to get to someplace dry and safe.

CHAPTER 3

Drawn to the glow of the city's lights reflecting off the clouds, I made my way into the more populated area and eventually ended up in the heart of the city. This was an older area of town. The buildings had been around for decades. Many of the alleys were still cobblestone. The curbs were short from multiple layers of road asphalt laid over each other. Aromas were plentiful, as I made my way down the streets. The corners of buildings were marked by a previous four-legged explorers.

I spent my first night on a doormat, inside a recessed entrance to a used bookshop, which was closed for the evening. Morning came with the sun shining. The light glistened off the parking meters, catching my good eye. Stretching, I loosened my joints then move to the hydrant at curbside. Leaning against it I relieved myself, then continued through the streets of this newfound city.

After some time, I found a large park where I felt some peace away from the cars and trucks moving about the streets. I was starting to get up in dog years by this time. My take was, that I had almost reached my nineth, maybe tenth birthday. I measured my steps, trying to stay out of harm's way. There were a few metal statues on large granite bases of men who had died but had done something important at one time or another. I found a comfortable place in the park where the walking paths crossed and I basked in the sun, resting beneath one on these monuments.

I was about thirty feet off the walking path, which was graced with an occasional fixed park bench. The benches had cement feet with dark green boards that were bolted in place for sitting on. There were few people in the park on this day, which was good for me, as I tended to draw a certain amount of attention due to my handicaps. Not sure how to categorize me as an example of a hard life or a carnival exhibit, they came to stare regardless of my feelings.

An older oriental man dressed in a black suit, sat down on the bench across from the statue I was resting under.

Shortly after, a woman passed by and said, "Good afternoon, Father!" As I looked in his direction, the gentleman smiled at me.

Another couple passed by a few minutes later greeting the man in the same way. I started feeling that he was different than the other people who were moving about. He sat there a full hour, eyes closed at times. Finally, he bowed his head and moved his hand to his head and shoulders, before getting to his feet and making his way toward me. Still having good hearing, I heard him say, "Amen." As he proceeded toward me, I turned my head in his direction so I could observe this man with my good eye. When he was within ten feet I stood up in a defensive move. He stopped in his tracks and began to talk softly to me. I felt a kindness about him. He reminded me of the man who played the harmonica many years earlier.

Moving in his direction I gave my best approachable look, yawned my high-pitched squeak and let him reach down to pet me. He crouched down, making our introduction easier by leveling the playing field.

"My name is Monsignor William Wei. My mother always said, 'Where there's Will there's a Wei!'" Then he laughed as if I understood.

"You look like you've had a difficult life, dog. Do you belong to anybody?" He asked, as if I would respond with an answer.

"I have a nice place to live if you'd like to get off of the streets," he added.

I'm not saying that I understood everything you humans uttered in my direction, but I could feel kindness as well as danger. I looked into his eyes and knew it would be good to follow him. It was early autumn, and the trees were beginning to lose their leaves. Soon, the wind and snow would visit for a time and although I had limited experience, I knew I needed a warm place. I needed some permanent shelter, like when I lived with the junkyard boss and the piano teacher.

I let out a happy bark, wagging my tail and followed the man in black down the street. He would stop now and then for a greeting with a handshake and usually a short conversation with someone passing by. I'd keep a few feet behind him and when he was engaged, I'd lean on a pole, wetting the sidewalk or sniff about the curb area adjacent to the road.

While I was deep in thought trying to determine who had marked a hydrant prior to me, a small van pulled up. Out came a guy in his late thirties with a snare pole. The monsignor was occupied talking to a young couple at the time. The animal control guy tried to slip the loop over my head, when at last, the monsignor came to my aid.

"Whoa, fella! That's my dog you're trying to confiscate!"

"Well Father, he's not wearing a collar. I thought him to be a stray," said the animal control officer.

"Oh, I see. I'll need to get that and his license," the monsignor replied. "He doesn't get out much."

"Good thing I'm wearing a collar," the monsignor joked, laughing loudly.

"What's his name, Father?"

"I, I . . . call him . . . Dog, so not to confuse him. Here, Dog," he said, as he went to one knee.

I obliged by coming over to his outstretched hand. Eyes were locked, while smiles were exchanged with the dogcatcher and the clergyman. The young man returned to his truck and drove away, with a short wave at the man of GOD. I followed close behind as we made our way to the rectory a few blocks further down the street. From that time on, I knew him as Father.

The church, rectory, and nun's quarters had been there for many years. Although appearing tired, it was still a very active parish. There was a grade school, in which classes were taught by nuns and lay teachers as well.

This was a nice place! The monsignor shared his living quarters with two other priests. They made up the spiritual guidance team, male division. During the day, there were two older, gray-haired women who cleaned, organized, and cooked for the three men. The first week at my new location, the monsignor took me to the veterinarian so I could get my shots to keep me legal. They gave me something for the fleas too! After the visit, I was rewarded with a collar and a tag that hung from it. Never having worn one before, I found it uncomfortable the first few weeks. After that, it became part of me.

I had been given the run of the place but stayed pretty much near the kitchen of the rectory or an adjacent closet off the back hall where my bed was. Bedrooms for the clergy were upstairs.

The backdoor off my bedroom which was a large closet, led to the alley behind the rectory and church. An adjacent door led downstairs. After some time, I learned how to transverse the steps to the cobblestones, where I'd explore up and down the alley way, leaving an occasional mark to say I had been there. Always mark one's territory. It was a dog's way of leaving a message. The rear of the local candy store was across the alley from the rectory, but I was much more interested in the rear of the meat market next door to the candy store. On occasion, I was given some scraps when the boss was with me.

Monsignor Wei made my life a pleasant life at Saint Joseph's. My last years were full of comfort and joy, giving me purpose, as I felt much the protector of the property. I knew deep down that I would not fare well in a fight with another, younger dog, but I could still bark and growl. I could sound the alarm, were it needed. With those actions I earned my keep, as well as felt some self-respect in those twilight years.

The two of us would take walks around the parish grounds when weather permitted. Many of the parishioners got to know me as a solid companion alongside the monsignor.

One very cold January night when the wind was full of vigor, the rear door blew open. It was snowing and the cold air was bitter to the bone. I rose to look outside and found that several inches of snow that had fallen.

With the door ajar, the snow now blocked the door from fully closing. Feeling safe that I wouldn't get locked out of the rectory, I ventured out on the landing and down the stairs looking around for a spot to pee. I propped myself against a dumpster and relieved myself. It was then that I spotted a figure making his way down the alley. I let out a low growl as he approached but something deep inside me said to allow this one access. I slowly returned inside and curled up in my bed.

I had my eyes on the door as this lone refugee entered. Kicking the snow away from the bottom of the door, he quietly closed it behind him. Before he took another step, he scanned the immediate area, then found the door to the rectory's basement which led to the church's basement. I heard his footsteps fade from the bottom stairs into the darkness. My thoughts were that he needed a place to stay. I had been there myself many times. I smacked my lips and dozed off to the sound of the wind outside but with one ear on standby. That was the last I saw of him until the next day.

The church's basement held the grade school cafeteria as well as a stage for presentations. Tables and chairs were positioned about for various gatherings. These included the kid's lunch program, Friday night fish fries, Christian youth groups, and catechism classes.

One late February morning I heard the woman who cooked for the priests crying about something. I rose from my bed, then entered the kitchen to an overwhelming sadness. After a few minutes of watching the humans, I realized that there had been what they call a *death*. The only time in my years there I took a leap in faith, as they say, and I negotiated my way up the stairs to the monsignor's bedroom. He was still in his sleep clothes and in his bed. He appeared silent, much like my old friend the piano teacher, the junkyard boss, and the harmonica man. He looked peaceful, as I whined a bit expressing my sadness. Returning to the kitchen for a drink of water, I hopped back to my bed and sunk my head down low. I thought, *I will miss him. He was a good boss.* Eventually, the group of humans was sure to settle down but for now my plan was to lay low, so as not to be stepped on.

I could see a pattern here with these humans. I had observed this with different animals as well, and I began to wonder when I too might find that permanent sleep. After all, I was literally half the dog I used to be. And yet, even with my missing parts, I was no less the dog that I started out at in this life. Perhaps I was even more blessed with my years of acquired knowledge. I learned along the way that there were both good and bad humans and animals alike.

My thoughts played on as the day progressed. Finally, near midday, I caught the smell of a couple of whole chickens roasting in the oven. For now, there was purpose, as my mind was cleared of all thoughts other than the filling of an empty stomach. I was sure to get some chicken as well as my dry dog food before the day was over.

I guess you could call me Lucky. In fact, call me blessed!

God's Ear!

THE GAVEL HIT THE aged, oak table which sounded that the meeting was going to start.

"Welcome everyone! My name is Skip. I'm an alcoholic."

The members greeted back in unison, "Welcome, Skip!"

Skip continued with "How It Works," chapter 5 of the Big Book,[1] as us alcoholics have come to call it.

This was my first meeting in years. I had gotten sober in 1990 and stayed that way for close to eleven years. Don't ask me why, but I ended up going out and doing additional research to verify that I indeed was an alcoholic. It started out innocently enough but like the small chunk of snow that falls from some evergreen bough high on a mountain, it quickly accumulates more snow, thus eventually creating an avalanche. I, too, propelled downward in total destruction. I found myself at the crossroads once again.

I listened to the litany as if I was in a dream state. My eyes scanned the room avoiding the other eyes but focusing on the makeup of the room. There were some spiritual pictures on the walls, as well as a plain cross. Children's artwork for the Christmas season was pinned to a corkboard. This indicated a day care center perhaps, at other times of the day in this room. The building housed many neighborhood events.

The paint on the walls was old, and the insulated pipes were pealing in places. My eyes passed the clock on the wall which had virtually stopped, as I sweated out the minutes of the meeting. I followed one pipe that ran across the front of the room and over the head of the chairperson. When my eyes had reached the spot directly over the heads of the alcoholics in the first row, I noticed an old piece of rope tied and hanging in a loop from that green-painted water pipe. A fleeting thought entered my mind, that it

1. Alcoholics Anonymous World Services, Inc., *Alcoholics Anonymous*.

was a hangman's noose. The only thing missing was my neck. I felt eyes on me while I had my head bent somewhat back, so I returned my focus to the meeting.

Someone behind me must had a full tank of elixir, because he or she was knocking a seasoned soldier as myself just about off my chair. No matter, they were at least trying to get sober. I sat there getting nervous, feeling that there were many eyes on me, and they were taking my inventory. I guess I didn't really want to get sober on this night. I needed a drink! The reality was that I also needed a place to warm up, to thaw out, and come up with a plan for the immediate future.

A few people shared their story after Skip shared, then the half hour cigarette break began as I came out of my trance. Warm enough, I slipped out of the door and down the street with no destination. As I was walking away someone shouted, "Come back again, friend!" A couple of hours later as night settled in, I began to feel frail.

The wind was punishing me again. Remember that mid-December wind accompanied by single digit temperatures? You would remember if you were from the North. It moves through your clothes and cuts at your flesh like so many razors. It works its way down beneath the flesh and plays havoc with your bones. Your tendons stiffen and your mind screams for shelter. You feel life disappearing from the ends of your appendages. Fingers, toes, ears, and your nose become senseless to their surroundings. This is where it gets serious, and you find refuge at any cost. And now it started to snow again. I tightened my navy blue knit hat to my head while I walked.

I had a warm spot picked out in a twenty-four-hour laundromat, but the cop that visited the place on his rounds didn't care for me hanging about without a load in the washer or dryer. I moved on after his second visit. I didn't want any trouble. Sitting the night in the slammer was not quite an option just yet.

I knew I couldn't go back into the meeting hall, where I had gone earlier in the evening. By now, the meeting was over and the building was locked up, so I continued down the pavement.

Reaching my fifty-year mark and being out on the street was beginning to sink in.

I needed desperately to find a place to stay. I needed to get some sleep. I simply could not push my body any further today. Being a bum in the year 2001 was no easy feat but it was the one job I could do with conviction.

There was no other job I wanted and, for that matter, had any interest in or could hold on to. I was a loser and with that, there was no denial.

Now, what I really needed was that drink! Get the head to stop thinking, talking, spinning! I wanted that dull, painless stupor, which I wore like the perfect business suit. That would make my day! I could have used a heavier coat as well. The kind that could hold a bottle in those deep pockets, but I couldn't find a Goodwill drop box to pilfer. This city was relatively new to me. I picked a bad time to head north again but I've heard timing is everything. Reality was trying to become my friend, but I would have none of it. The opposition was the group inside my head which needed to be silenced. This was the chamber group that sat in the center of my mind, playing the same sad song. *Depression and worry, low self-esteem, too damn cold to dream*, went the song in my head.

GOD, I hate myself. Why can't I just die? went the depressing song in my mind. Then I thought, *There you go Harold, feeling sorry for yourself again. You poor, unfortunate being.*

Always ready to whine. Wine! Now, there's a thought! Ha! Ha! Much better, you damn fool. Just get silly in the head and the cops will pick you up eventually, then at least you'll have a warm cell. I'm just not ready for that yet. Geez, I'm freezing and I'm thirsty.

I continued down one of the alleys of the city, looking for anything that might be inviting. One alley after another I passed through rendered nothing warm. I was walking through those valleys of forgotten backdoors. Each alley was much the same as the last until I entered the one on Seventh Avenue and State Street. This alley had some promise. It almost seemed like it was inviting me. Large dumpsters and war-damaged, plastic garbage receptacles from overzealous sanitation engineers were behind each building. Some were overflowing with yesterday's dinner scraps from a fine diner. The meat market, candy store, and other businesses filled the remaining stretch down this cobblestone alley. The opposite side of the alley was owned by a church.

An old dog with one less front leg than he was birthed with watched me as I made my way past the back of several buildings. All I could think of was, *trees and fire hydrants must be a challenge. Well, we all got our problems, but he was lucky to be alive.* As he looked me over, I thought, he was in no shape to be outside. I wondered if he had a home. He wore his scars proudly but looked like a loser, a loser of many fights. I briefly identified with him. Some movement beyond the dog caught my attention. An open door swung on its hinges in the wind, slapping dully against the snow that kept it from closing tight and locking. It beckoned me in from the cold and I wasn't about to argue.

The dog hobbled up the concrete stairs and entered ahead of me, disappearing into the darkness. When he had gotten to the landing, I noticed he had an eye missing as well. As I grabbed the doorknob and entered the threshold, I took my foot and I cleared away enough of the snow to close the door. The storm moaned at my gesture. Gathering that the animal knew his way around this place and didn't bark, I did not foresee him as a threat. This looked like the rectory next to the church. I continued carefully into building, taking a scan of the area to make sure there were no other eyes on me. Safe so far, I slithered into the hallway like the snake I was. The interior heat caressed my tired body. I silently said, *Ahh.*

A faint yawning whine came from an adjacent room. The dog let me know he was watching. He apparently thought that I, too, needed shelter.

Listening intently, I heard nothing else. I found a doorway and descended eight steps into the darkness then turned left. I moved toward the night-light on the opposite side of the room. As I made my way through this basement, I found another door which placed me in a larger basement. A couple of weak night-lights illuminated what appeared to be a cafeteria for the grade school and sometimes bingo hall, all in the dormant stage. Looking around the room there were posters of saints and religious sayings hanging on the walls. An artificial Christmas tree filled one corner of the hall. A large, faded painting of the Last Supper adorned one of the other walls. A crucifix was hung at the back of the stage behind the podium. Adding up my observations, I figured I was in the church's basement.

Jesus, poor souls, and all things holy, were my reflections at that moment. Still, I was out of the cold and maybe wine wasn't too farfetched of an idea! *They do use wine,* the voices in my head confirmed.

Noises!

I thought I heard someone coming, so I slipped up the stairs at the other end of the hall. When I reached the top, I found myself in the vestibule of the church. There were three soft amber lights positioned over the doorways to the church interior. As I entered the body of the church, I saw the flicker of two votive candles burning in a wrought iron stand near the altar. They were at the end of their lives. I vaguely remembered my mother lighting a candle for her grandmother when I was a kid, then kneeling and praying for a few minutes. The glass containers the candles were in were colored red, while others were green back then. These were red with a few purple candleholders as well. I wondered if the purple candleholders were for more important people or carried a higher prayer. The church was softly lit from large ceiling fixtures, which hung from long black chains.

Lost souls, that was it! She was praying for her grandmother's soul, I remembered.

The faint smell of incense hung in the air, along with something I cannot find the right words for. It was comforting and yet, mysterious at the same time. Right of the podium where the priest would talk was a manger and statues of the birth of the Christ Child.

I guessed it to be around one thirty on a Saturday morning. Through my muddled thinking, I thought it to be several days before Christmas. It had been a long time since I celebrated any holy holiday, although my upbringing had started out with connection to the church. I even remember trying out to be an altar boy, but I failed to show up for a mass I was scheduled to serve. That was the end of my altar boy career. It was still storming outside, and I could hear the wind blowing past the stained glass windows in the church. I laid down on an oak pew and fell fast asleep.

Hours later, I heard a door open somewhere near the altar and the sound startled me. As I rose, an old woman appeared and started dusting the altar at the front of the church. She had a vacuum cleaner with her, as well as other cleaning supplies. The cleaning woman started the vacuum up and I stayed silent in the shadows for a time. When she stopped vacuuming and retreated back into the hallway, I moved quietly to the aisle along the outside wall of the church. Slipping into a booth with a carved, ornate doors and dark, purple velvet curtains, I sat down quickly, took a deep breath, and held it in. Listening to see if the old woman had heard me, I waited. Only the faint sound of the wind outside from the blizzard touched my ears. My eyes were heavy, and my body exhausted from the weather, as well as the disrupted sleep.

My thoughts reorganized themselves on the top shelf of my mind and I realized I was in a confessional. I thought of a time long ago when I was pulled by the arm to church. My mother took me there and she made me tell the priest that I had stolen a candy bar. She told me it would be good for my soul if I did this. I must have been about seven or eight years old. After my mother made such a big deal about it, I went through the motions to survive. After failing as an altar boy, I never returned to that church or any other, unless forced on a Sunday. I did remember seeing a few scenes out of the movies over the years, depicting the goings on of the church, but it was never as I remembered it.

Better tell or go to hell, ran through my mind as I drifted off to a guarded sleep. Unaware in my sleep, I hit a switch with my shoulder and flipped the light on outside the confessional. This meant the priest was available for confession. I dreamt of days when I was still married. I hid bottles of vodka all around the house. They were tucked into winter coat pockets, under stairs, inside the Shop-Vac, and various places in the garage. The ex-wife was a great detective and found most of the cache. I even tied a string on one bottle and nailed it on the far side of a tree at the back of our lot. In my dream, I searched and searched the premises for a drink but only came up with empty bottles on my Easter egg hunt of sorts.

I was startled into consciousness by the sound of someone kneeling on the opposite side of the chamber I was in. A great sweat formed as I gathered my marbles back into the bag. There was a small sliding door with a dark screen in place and I heard a small voice say, "Bless me Father, for I have sinned. My last confession was last Saturday. I'm really sorry for being bad Father."

Before I could think, I heard my mouth say, "What did you do, kid?"

"Slide the wooden window to the side Father, then I can hear you better."

"Oh! Oh yeah, kid. I forgot."

The boy continued by saying, "I stole these two metal cars from the variety store, Father. I'm afraid I'm going to go to hell or at least purgatory! What should I do, Father?"

"Chri . . . ! I mean, have you still got the cars, kid?" I thought, *I can't say Christ in a defamatory way!*

"Yes, Father. They're still in my pocket."

"Well kid . . . I think that you'd better take them back and tell the store owner what you did. Tell him that you are very sorry. Let him know that it won't happen again."

"You think so, Father, and are there any prayers for me to say?"

"Oh yeah! Say some prayers kid. Say ten prayers and don't steal no more! Christmas will be here soon, and you might get something better than those cars."

"OK, Father. Thanks!"

"Yeah, kid. I mean . . . go in peace."

Jesus! I exclaimed in my head and then realized that wouldn't do either, unless I was truly calling on him. *What the hell did I just do? I need to get out of here and darn quick before I run into company.*

Just then I heard someone enter from the other side of the enclosure. It seemed like I was caught in the middle. I slid the window thingy back a little on this new side and heard an old lady say, "Bless me, Father, for I have sinned. I cursed the grave of my late husband, Father."

Beads of sweat started to form on my forehead again. As I tried to gather my composure, I said, "And why on earth did you do that?!"

"Because he left me all alone and I miss him so very much. My life is empty now and I feel I have no reason to go on, Father. I wake at night because I think I hear him snoring, but I'm all alone, so I make a cup of coffee and sit at the table where we sat so many times before." Her voice quivered as she added, "I cry for hours, Father."

I told her, "I think he would be very hurt if he saw you wasting the rest of your life away. It is not very good to be angry with him, when there was nothing he could do to alter GOD's wishes. I'm sure," I went on, "that GOD has a purpose for you still being here. Listen! Why don't you come back this afternoon, Missus? There is a . . . a holiday bake sale, yeah, a bake sale."

There was a sign in the basement this morning, I remembered.

"Bring something that you have baked and get to know some of the people. It might help you to shake off the blues, Missus."

"Thank you, Father, you are very kind. Are you new here? I don't recognize your voice," she said, with a renewed hope in her speech.

"Yes! I'm Father Harold and I'm visiting from Poughkeepsie," I lied as grape size beads of sweat ran down my forehead. "Now go and do a rosary or two, Missus. Go with GOD."

Go lady, go . . . please go! Now, I'll need to go to confession! I need to anyway.

As she left, I thought, *what a hypocrite! Go with GOD. Really!? When was the last time I went with GOD or even thought about GOD? Damn! I mean, darn! I'll be lucky not to get struck down by lightening or end up in jail! I gotta get out of here!*

I poked my head out of the door and saw a woman in her early thirties. She looked worn out and she too was crying. My guess was that she had been crying for some time by the exhausted stare that went along with her tears.

Darn! She's getting up!

I pulled my head back in to the confessional like a prairie dog into its hole and froze. A moment, two moments, and she entered the adjoining chamber. Silently, we both waited, each in our own darkness. Minutes passed by like clouds on a hot, windless day. Then I remembered! I slid the door slowly open to the sound of, "Bless me, Father . . ." and she begins to sob.

"Yes?" I replied.

"I have been seeing another man, Father, and I'm a married woman. I don't know what to do." *The sobbing continued,* "I know I have sinned against the church and GOD Almighty, but my heart is alive, and it reaches out! What can I possibly do Father?"

Good grief! What the hell can I say to this woman? I couldn't hold one relationship together, let alone two!

"Listen, my child."

Boy, it was getting pretty thick in this little space I was hiding in.

"I'm not sure just what you should do, but here is a suggestion. Obviously, you cannot live with both of these men, so why not try living without both of them, and after a while, GOD will perhaps guide you in the right direction."

LORD! I wondered if I had said that or what!?

She sounded like she was beginning to absorb what I had shared with her, because her crying was starting to slow down to sniffles. I added that "GOD is all forgiving, so try to do what I have suggested and see if things will straighten out for you. Now go and light a candle for each man."

And please light one for me too, my heart pleaded.

I mumbled my interpretation of a blessing of absolution, and she left. *Dear GOD,* were my thoughts. *Yes! Dear GOD! What a tough job GOD must have, if this is what one of his priests must go through.*

Several more people entered with minor infractions. I dismissed them with abundant prayers to say, along with some basic street wisdom when, from my guess, a very nervous teenage boy enters. I take him for sixteen or seventeen by his faint outline through the screen. His first words are "Father, I'm in big trouble. I need your help! Pray for me please!"

"What is it my son?" I responded, now fully into my role.

"Father . . . I think . . . I just killed a man!" the boy stammered and then continued with his story.

"I, I robbed a small grocery store and the old man . . . I thought he was going for a gun, from behind the counter . . . so, I shot and ran! I ran and ran . . . finally, I ran into the church. I was hiding in the alley for some time, when I figured I'd better make my peace with GOD and came into the church. I needed to confess my sins before the cops take me down."

"Listen son, it might not be as bad as you think! Did you see the old man fall? Maybe you missed? Maybe he's hurt? If you keep running, it will get ugly and maybe you'll go down in a shoot-out. Do you want it all to end this way? You're at the place of decisions, young man. This is a major crossroad in your life. You must decide to run or turn yourself in. One path will surely be shorter."

"I'm scared, Father!"

"I know and understand your fears, young man. We are all scared at one time or another in our lives. That is why GOD never leaves us. We forget about GOD, but GOD waits patiently to guide us through each storm. Give GOD a chance by turning yourself in please. After all, you don't want to hurt anyone, or you would not be here. Please leave the gun if you still have it on you. Then I want you to go up to the rectory and there will be another priest who will guide you through this."

"The gun is in the alley, in the trash container, Father," the rattled boy responded.

"I must stay here and finish confessions for those who remain. Please tell Father what you have told me, and he will accompany you to retrieve the gun. Do not retrieve the gun alone. Go to Father first. He will help you through this difficult time with the authorities.

"Now go with GOD and know that he loves you."

He left and I could only wonder if he had followed my instructions. I had to admit, I was a little shook with the idea that he could have shot me too. Tossing what I had said around in my mind, I spoke quietly to GOD and asked for his help and his forgiveness. I peeked out of the confessional like a timid rat, and it appeared that the church was finally empty. There were someone's fading footsteps and a door closing, then silence.

Time to split!

I moved into the aisle turning toward the basement door, then changed my mind and moved toward the side entrance of the church. As I opened it, I ran right into the monsignor. "Excuse me, son," he said, "I'm late for confessions. I was on call and had to go to the hospital for someone in need. Anyone waiting friend? Did you need to see me yourself?"

"Don't think so, Father, and no, GOD and I are on good terms today but thanks for asking. Merry Christmas to you!"

I kept my head down as I screwed my knit hat onto my noggin and walked briskly down the cement stairs and across the street. As I took a look back, a smile filled my mouth, as I saw the teenager at the rectory door being let in by another priest. He had listened.

Thank GOD. Yeah! Thank GOD!

I waltzed down the sidewalk with a renewed positive attitude. The thought of a nice breakfast entered my mind, as it was nearing nine o'clock. It had been a very long night and morning. Even the dog I had saw in the wee hours of the morning looked better to me. He barked towards me from the alley on the other side of the street. Reaching into my pants pocket I was surprised when I located a twenty-dollar bill.

Odd, I thought I had a five, I mused.

Yeah! Breakfast! Some bacon and eggs come to mind! Don't really feel like a drink today. Maybe another AA meeting tonight.

I began whistling an old tune, looking up to the heavens.

"Joy to the World"[2] . . . as I blended back into life once again.

---

2. Watts and Handel, "Joy to the World."

Letting Go of Earth

By the world's standards, my life was partly cloudy with rain in the forecast, or at least that's how I felt inside. I had experienced marriage, raised a child to six years old, and divorced. My daughter went with her mother to a different town to start over. I get to see her several times a year. I got married again and lost my second wife in an unfortunate car accident. I was in my late thirties at this place in time. I was alive, but with little to no purpose. I was given a few years of solitude to work through my losses and find a new direction. By that, I mean there were no life shattering experiences in the past twenty-four months and it allowed me time to figure what my life was all about. I seem to have failed the course.

After a couple of Christmas's passed by and I got over feeling sorry for myself for being alone, I settled down into a familiar pattern of going to work and going home, going to work, and going home. Life swung methodically like a pendulum with an occasional trip to the Walmart or a competitive grocery store. Then there was the occasional taking in a movie at the mall. Most recently I had begun to branch out, trying to break the pattern which was affecting me like many of my fellow zombies walking around this world. It was the middle November.

It was a late Friday afternoon after work, so I drove over to the mall and decided to take in the latest flick. I love movies! After I made my choice of pictures to see, I had some time to kill before the movie started, so I walked the mall for a while. When I approached the candle store, I shifted to the opposite side of the aisle where a coffee and bagel shop had recently opened. For some reason my nose was sensitive today and the candle smells gagged me. The rest of me was worn down after five days of work. I had the going-to-the-movies-alone syndrome, which constantly repeated itself on so many Fridays before.

It came to me in a dark dream a few nights earlier, that I had watched all the movies the theater was showing. In my nightmare of sorts, I feared having a week on my hands before the movies changed and new movies presented themselves. I was afraid to not have anything to do. Quite silly when I thought about it.

As I proceeded through the mall, there was a slight slap on my sneaker. Looking down, I found that my shoe had come untied. Spotting an open seat on the upcoming bench, I asked an elderly woman if anyone was sitting there. She began to laugh but beckoned me with her hand to sit down.

"I don't see anyone, but you never know, there could be someone sitting there!" she shared, laughing through her remarks.

Taking a hard look at the bench, I figured it was empty, but she did catch me by surprise, and found myself scanning the blank space for an occupant of any size. A momentary feeling of foolishness came over me. I would have named myself *Gullible Travels*, for I was easily sucked into things like what just occurred. I tied my shoe and righted myself.

"How is it going today?" I asked.

"It's OK," she responded. Then she looked away and about, as if she were checking for listeners. She returned her focus and looked back at me, saying in a whispered voice, "Imagine you're on a ball spinning through space."

"What? What do you mean?" I responded, in a surprised way at the comment.

"Just look around. You'll understand, eventually." And she began to laugh again. It was a joyous laugh that almost tickled a soul. It was that laugh, which stands out in a laugh track, over the rest of the cackling. Her attitude reminded me of Mrs. Claus, but looked nothing like the image I held in my mind of the aforementioned. She was a short and thin woman who carried a little belly. Dressed in a dark blue winter jacket, she sported a sweatshirt beneath it. I noted in my mind her dark brown slacks and brown loafers with bright yellow socks. She wore large, oval bifocals down on her nose. Her hair was more salt than pepper by an eighty to twenty percent ratio. It was cut shorter than shoulder length and flipped under. The sweatshirt had "Save the Planet" on the front and was of a forest green in color with an image of the Earth beneath the saying. I assumed she was for a greener Earth. Her hands caught my eyes. I wanted to reach out and hold them. For the life of me I cannot explain why.

I got to my feet, gave her a look, and shook my head muttering, "Too much crack pipe, lady?"

This only made her laugh harder.

"You'll have to sweeten that bitter attitude, young man, or you'll be sorry. There is much in store for you."

Her voice faded as I walked across the food court toward the theater.

Young man? I pondered the comment thinking, *I was in my late thirties.* I guess that was still young from her perspective. Then there was that weird comment she made.

Imagine you're on a ball spinning through space. I chewed on that line mentally as I walked.

It kind of bugged me, like strolling through the graveyard at night. It was just a statement, but it felt spooky to me. Fingers on the shoulders spooky! Shaking my reality, it brought me out of my box, my safe zone where I was comfortable. I looked up through the mall's glass atrium just before I bought my movie ticket. Darkness began to settle in for the night. Musing over what she had said made me take a different perspective of the sky on this mid autumn afternoon. I saw the darkness beyond, then started to think of all that was in the universe. Zombie walking to my seat, I stared at the screen and answered the same movie trivia questions that flashed on it for the past six months. Daydreaming, I visualized all the people of the world sticking up from this blue ball we lived on. Much like the trees, we too were vertical but mobile.

Imagine . . . spinning through space kept echoing through my mind.

The previews of coming attractions blared across the screen, then the snack bar commercial, finally, the silence your cellphone speech, and shortly thereafter the movie began. I entered the fantasy and lost two hours of reality in the process. Mildly satisfied I returned home, seated myself in front of the computer, and went online to visually scan my usual stops but nothing interested me. A pause at the refrigerator netted me a cold pork chop and a cranberry juice. A few more snacks and the twenty-four-hour news on the TV brought me near enough to bedtime.

My stomach made demonic sounds, as I thought, *I should never have eaten all that junk just before bed.*

My head worked the pillow trying to nest, but my mind was still stuck on those words that the old woman had uttered. *Imagine you are on a ball* . . . it was as if she were toying with me when she spoke. I couldn't shake it though and lay there with eyes wide open. I wondered if she put a curse on me or something. A small daddy longlegs moved across the ceiling as I listened to my heart pulsate.

An hour must have passed by when I finally got up and looked out the window at the sky. As my stomach made another remark, I decided from where I stood that I couldn't get enough of what I was looking for. My next move was to go outside, where I stood on the porch in my underwear. Gazing the across the horizon I saw the glow of the city then I looked straight up.

There were stars in a very clear universe with only a sliver of a moon. Time nor the cold was important to me, as I scanned the cosmos for several minutes. Returning inside, I pondered some more over the old woman's conversation, although briefly. I guess I never thought about it before, but the old woman was correct. I was standing on a ball, spinning through space and was as blind to that fact as the many people who passed me by in daily life. Finally chilled, I returned to bed with that thought in my mind. It gave way to eventual sleep.

Daybreak was a welcome sight, dissipating the dream state from my mind. I felt a surge of energy and light on my feet as I hit the coffee switch to start the morning ritual. Shower time brought the pot to four cups worth of brew, and I scarfed down a bowl of instant oatmeal to get the body recycling. I went back on the internet to find out a little about the solar system, the universe, and what lies beyond. I lost my patience after several failed attempts to reconnect after getting knocked offline. I gave up and returned downstairs to read. Filling the rocker, I crossed my legs and began flipping pages. I was about halfway through an article in a magazine when I looked up. My left leg which I had been crossed over my right, was now suspended in the air! Dropping the monthly, I stood up almost falling over as I brought the floating appendage back to earth. I found myself pushing down on my knee, holding it to the floor, but when I let go it was fine. I thought, *You're cracking up, man!* I swore to myself that my leg felt like a helium filled balloon. Absolutely weightless!

Since it was the beginning of the weekend, I had time to pull myself together as there was nothing on my calendar. I went for a ride but avoided the mall area which was too busy on Saturdays. I felt jumpy. I had all this pent-up energy. Stopping into my local fitness center, which I had been deemed "missing in action," I reintroduced myself to the guy who was tending the sweatshop. He looked back at me like I was a total stranger. Scanning the room, I counted three other people doing their physical rituals and hoisted myself on to the stationary bike. I rode it for twenty minutes, working myself into a lather. The attendant kept giving me looks like, *I think I remember you. You were much thinner the last time I saw your body in here. I hope you're not going to pass out!* I left out of there with a quick goodbye.

It looked like rain or possibly snow might be on the way, but I still needed something to do. Those dark, heavy clouds that were just overhead added an ominous touch to the day. I stopped by my apartment and took a second shower. Refreshed, I returned to my Saturday morning adventure. I had a feeling similar but not quite the same as being on amphetamines. Extreme anxiousness comes to mind. I got into my car and headed out of town to one of the surrounding apple orchards. When I arrived, I got a handheld basket and moved out among the trees for some nice Honeycrisp. They were my favorites! It was the very end of the season, so the trees were almost bare. I got a dozen in the basket they provided. Moving around helped this impatient feeling to subside a little.

I took my bounty to the checkout in the small store at the front of the orchard. They sold a variety of harvest goodies including cherries, cheese, and sausages. Looking around, I picked up a cherry pie still warm from the oven. Unlocking my car, I put my bag of apples in the backseat on the floor and the pie on the other side on the seat. I was just starting to back out of my space, when through my rearview mirror I saw an older woman carrying a large bag of apples. The bag split and her red orbs were all over the gravel lot. Hesitating for just a moment, I tossed several scenarios in my mind. They seemed to all blend together. I decided to continue on my way, although I had no immediate place I needed to be. Oddly, I found myself driving forward, back into the parking spot and turning the car off. I stepped out and asked, "Do you need any help, ma'am?"

This was a weak way of saying, *Please release me from this obligation.*

She looked up and said, "I'll be fine."

At that point I wanted to get back into the car, but I started to feel this exasperating anxiousness well up in me again. As I turned toward the store, I began to feel better and decided to get a couple of empty bags from the proprietor. Returning to help the lady, I joined her in picking up the apples. The two of us bagged half of the orbs in each of the two bags. I followed her to her car with one of the bags in hand and placed it on the floor in the back seat. She was very grateful and thanked me as I returned to my own vehicle.

"GOD bless you, young man."

"You are very welcome," I responded.

I waved back, slipped into my front seat, and drove off. A bit of self-analysis had me thinking that in the past, my life was too busy to stop everything and help someone like that. Today, I felt the rewards of taking that time out of my life to assist another human being. *What did it cost me but a few minutes of my time?* I mused.

The rest of Saturday was uneventful. I found refuge in the confines of my apartment the remainder of the day. When I awoke Sunday morning, I was feeling refreshed until I saw my blankets draped over my legs like a tent. Both legs were suspended toward the ceiling. Yelping, out loud, yes, yelping, I rolled onto the floor. Standing upright, I seemed to be OK.

Maybe I just imagined my legs in the air was the thought I wrestled with. Must have still been dreaming, I concluded. I still felt like my internal engine was running fast. After a shower, then bouncing around between the walls of my apartment, I watched the news over a bowl of cereal. The dishes needed to be washed, so I did that along with a quick vacuuming of the living room. I decided to go to the mall after I ate some lunch. *Sunday might have less of a crowd, and she might be there,* was my thinking. Jamming a peanut butter and jelly sandwich down with a milk chaser, found myself ready for adventure. I needed to find the old woman. I had questions as to who she was and if she had done something to me. Feeling like I wronged her, I decided I needed to apologize for the crack pipe remark.

Must be a curse, I thought.

On Sunday, the mall opened at noon. I parked my car then sat for ten minutes waiting for the mall guy to unlock the doors. Eventually, I saw the security guard come by the entrance and he opened the mall for business. Several other assorted people were waiting to go in besides myself. I waited until the pack of anxious shoppers entered, then I too followed the herd. Walking up and down the main aisle of the mall, I found no sign of her. I returned to the center hub where the fountain and the information desk were. Continuing my search up and down the east and west corridors in the mall, I still could not locate the mysterious woman. When I reached the east end, people were lining up for the movie theater to open. I scanned the lines of people but still no old woman. I decided to sit down on a bench, hoping she would come by. Twenty minutes later she came toward where I was sitting.

"Looking for me, youngster?" she said, as she approached.

I replied with a yes and told her how sorry I was for being a smart aleck the other day. She accepted my apology with a smile. Just when I was getting ready to question her about what was happening to me, she excused herself telling me she was going to the lady's room. I sat patiently for another twenty minutes, then got up and walked toward the restrooms. After some time, I asked another woman who was going in to use the facilities if she could see if an older, thin woman in a dark blue winter jacket was in the restroom. I waited patiently outside of the facility. She returned after ten minutes or so and said the restroom was empty. I thanked her and returned to my car thinking, *She never really said she was coming back. I just assumed she would.* I was baffled as I drove back to my apartment, still with a head full of questions.

My radio alarm went off on Monday morning to the sound of old rock and roll. The music warmed my body's engine as I lay there. A blink or two passed, then I opened my eyes realizing another weekend had disappeared. As my senses began to focus, I was startled to find that both of my arms were pointed toward the ceiling as I lay flat on my back. They were up in the air like they were suspended by balloons! I let out a kind of howl this time, as I jumped from the sheets to the floor. The movement restored them to my sides and I turned the radio off. This was too darn freaky! I needed answers as to what was going on. My thoughts returned to the old woman at the mall once again. I felt she was the cause somehow, but the mall was closed, and I needed to be at work. There was no other way I could connect with her, but I knew I had to try. Even running into her again was a long shot. She would not give me the slip again. So, this encounter would have to wait until later in the day. I would need to take care to watch myself, in the event that this floating thing happened in front of my coworkers.

Traffic was light as I made my way toward work. I was behind my normal pace, and I hated to be late for my job. When I turned at the street corner, I saw this wheelchair tipped over and an old black man on the ground. He was struggling to get his chair upright. Missing his left leg at the knee made the task almost impossible. I pulled over and parked my car.

"Here! Let me give you a hand," I pleaded.

"Thanks! I hit the broken curb wrong as I was trying to get across the street. Tipped my rig over. I was heading to the VFW post."

"Ex-military?" I questioned, as I handed him his hat which told of his unit and when he served overseas.

"Yeah! Vietnam, in the Army, a long time ago."

"My late uncle was over there in 1969," I responded. "They say he seemed different when he got back stateside."

"Yeah . . . some of us wear our scars on the outside, others on the inside, but we all are marked by war," he shared with a faraway look in his eyes.

I got his wheelchair upright, then proceeded to lift him from under the arms into his ride. I was anxious to get going as he continued his story and how he stepped on a pressure device that exploded and took his leg off. He had caught my ear, as now, I listened intently. Grabbing the handles on the chair, I rolled him across the street to his destination. I found myself welling up inside.

He thanked me saying, "Quite a few cars drove right by like I didn't exist. Can't figure people out these days. It's like they have no heart and soul anymore. At least I wasn't robbed. I appreciate that you took the time to help an old man out, friend."

I thanked him for serving our country, crossed the street and got back in my car. I lost about fifteen minutes, but I gained a good experience as I finished my drive to work.

Maybe it was because I am in a fast-moving business that has a lot of interruptions throughout the day, or the fact that I was focused while I worked, but nothing happened that I might call out of the ordinary. Well, I did hear my foot hit the underside of the desk later in the day when I started to tire out. I dismissed it as just stretching my hamstrings.

I took my customary shower in the men's locker facilities after my shift and felt extremely light. I laughed to myself that I had removed the dirt as well as my clothes and that made me feel buoyant. Kidding no one, I was baffled. Dressing quickly, I moved out of the locker room and down to the parking lot. I had my mind focused on one thing and that was to find that old lady. Trying to maintain my composure, I began my drive over to the mall but the closer I got to my destination the more hurried I became internally.

I parked crooked over the lot stripes, jumped out of the car, and jogged into the mall's food court. Walking briskly past the fast-food choices, down around the fountain at the left spur of the mall, and past the candle shop, I spotted her. She was approaching the same bench where I had stopped to tie my sneaker several days earlier. The old woman managed to sit down before I got there. She had one of those canvas tote bags that replaced paper and plastic, which now rested against her leg. Never raising her head, she knew it was me and simply said, "You're back."

"Things are different now. What the hell is happening to me?" I said through clenched teeth.

"You've begun to realize," she said, as a matter-of-fact.

"Realize what? That I'm getting lighter? That I find parts of my body floating in the air? What is going on here? What did you do to me?"

"Floating?! I only awakened you from the dream. Now you need to do something about it," she told me as she cackled, laughing loudly.

"You should see the look on your face right now," and she laughed some more with this robust joy she carried in her small frame.

I was angry and I reached out to grab her jacket as she turned away, but my hand floated above her, missing the mark.

She turned around quickly and said, "That won't do. Go on now and leave me be. We both have work to do. You'll understand . . . in time. Here, read this," as she handed me a sheet of paper out of her tote bag. It was a flyer that said in big bold letters, "Missing:" with a name, age, and picture of a young girl. Faith was her name as I crumpled the paper into my pocket in a dismissive way.

I was a mix of anger and bewilderment. At the time, I could not understand why I was so upset and frustrated. I didn't know what to say or what to do. Frozen for a moment, I just stood there and watched her blend into the crowd with the canvas bag in hand.

Seating myself on the bench again, I thought of what a stupid thing I just did. Losing my cool with an old woman was not only inappropriate but foolish as well. I felt momentarily ashamed as I went over the brief encounter in my mind. Then it struck me. She did say that I would figure it out in time. Those words gave me some hope and I got to my feet. Hope was a long-lost friend, and I greeted its return with a warm feeling inside. Home seemed like a good place to hide, so I returned there. I turned on the television when I got on my couch. The television was more of a distraction in the background than anything thing else.

A favorite scripture from the book of Hebrews 11:1 kept echoing in my mind. *"Now faith is the assurance of things hoped for, the conviction of things unseen."*[1]

1. Hebrews 11:1 RSV.

Those words hadn't crossed my mind since I was chasing GOD through some revival meetings I had attended some eight years earlier. Those days, I found solace in the Bible or at least having it nearby.

After fifteen or twenty minutes of commercials I was sound asleep. I dreamt I was running in and out of a burning building but only to save good-looking people. They were all those types that have the drawn faces and portray zombies on the clothing runway of life. There was also a woman in gray fuzzy slippers and a pink and gray plaid bathrobe. She had enough curlers in her hair to contact the International Space Station and kept pleading for me to save her. I ignored the curler-ladened woman for a gaunt, hot redhead.

The more models I saved the lighter I became, until finally I was holding on to the door jamb because my body was floating away. I looked down at a rat that had been hurt by falling debris. There were singe marks on its coat, and it looked up at me with, yes, sad eyes. I reached out with one hand and picked up the rodent from the smoking rubble, and I immediately fell to the ground. I put the critter safely on the lawn. Maybe it was bouncing my head off the porch that did it, but I realized that woman with the curlers was still in the building screaming. I ran into the flames and smoke, crying out to her, "I'm here to save you, I'm here to save you!" What I heard back, haunted me.

"You're too late. I'm a lost opportunity!" And then there was silence. I sat directly up in bed, swinging my feet to the floor. Sweat was running off me like I was infected with malaria. Frightened by this dream, I sat for the longest time just staring straight ahead. Walking to the couch, I sat my body down. When I looked at the coffee table, there was the crumbled sheet of paper the old woman gave me. Flattening it out with both hands, I took a longer look at it and realized it was a picture of a nine-year-old girl named Faith. She had been missing for three days according to the flyer. *Poor girl,* I thought. *I wonder what could have happened to her.*

CHAPTER 2

The next few days were quiet. The Thanksgiving holiday was a week away, as I found myself driving through the downtown area of my little town on an early afternoon. Parking in a free lot I decided to walk the main street. I was still pent up with energy which seemed to ebb and flow over the past week. When I became self-centered, it appeared I would have these attacks of antigravity and find my appendages drifting about. However, when I reached out in a caring fashion toward anyone or anything, I came back to what I would call normal or grounded. It sounds bizarre but that's how it played out.

Minutes passed by as I walked aimlessly down one street then up the next. There was no destination in mind. I came around a corner and walked into three tough teens picking on an individual I might describe as being a bit challenged mentally. On any given day I would have scooted to the other side of the street because of the odds. I tried religiously to avoid all confrontations. Today however, I picked up my pace and found myself walking directly up to these people. This picking on the helpless rubbed me the wrong way. I stood there, staring at them without saying a word.

"Hey dude, can we help you?" The tallest of the three spouted in my direction, all the while bobbing his head like a pigeon. He was a magnet's dream. Pierced tongue, ears, lower lip, and eyebrow adorned his head in a variety of shapes and sizes. I wondered if this was some ancient form of intimidation taken from the animal kingdom but brought to a new level. Then I realized animals do not do that to themselves. Perhaps, he had a secret desire to be a Christmas tree. I wondered how he would look in another forty years. I wasn't impressed nor shaken by his appearance. I had seen more than enough carnival characters in my lifetime.

"Yes!" I responded. "I've come to guide my friend to a better place."

"Say what?" was the response of the short and obese member of the trio as he wrinkled his brow trying to understand me. He sported hardware in one pierced nostril and a miniature hockey puck in each earlobe. It was the stench drifting off his stained clothes which wobbled my knees briefly.

"I said, he is going with me to a better place," as the three of them circled the two of us.

"And what place would that be, dude?" the first one asked.

"The house of GOD," was my reply and they all looked puzzled, as if I had filled their heads with some kind of bewilderment. I remembered the tower of Babel story in the Good Book and how it told of the confusion of languages. These guys were out of their league without a guidebook. Puzzlement gave way to a blank slate.

"Awe, let's go. This guy's a drag anyway," the third one chided as the other two looked on. They wandered away down the block mumbling under their breaths. I couldn't help but notice the posted sign on the telephone poll they passed, which read, "Missing: Faith . . ."

She was still gone, I reflected.

"What's your name buddy?" I asked the young man with whom I was left with. He told me it was Andrew, and he was going to his residence up the street. He explained that others lived there as well, learning about how to be responsible. He said that in time, some of the people advanced out of there to live on their own without supervision. I told him I would walk with him if he didn't mind and he said, "That would be nice, Mister."

"What is your name, Mister?" he asked.

I replied, "It's Jeffery."

Pointing at the sign on the post he said, "You should find Faith, Jeffery."

I looked back over my shoulder and mumbled, "Yeah, faith in something."

I guessed he was in his early twenties but acted closer to a twelve-year-old. He stopped for a full minute at every street corner whether there was anything coming or not. I guessed it to be a good thing.

"I need to be careful," he told me. "I was hit by a car a long time ago. N-now I look both ways."

When I delivered him to the door of the house, he grabbed my hand and shook it very firmly, thanking me. Then he looked me in the eyes before he went in and said, "You have nice hands, Mr. Jeffery, and thank you, thank you!"

I took a slow walk back to my car thinking about everything that had happened in the previous days. It was cold and the first hints of snow began to fill the air with the tiniest of flakes. Winter weather wasn't too far away nor was Christmas. The holiday season had always been such a special time for me as a child. Years of commercialism, many struggles in my life including divorce, bad decisions, and then the loss of my second wife, caused me to grow bitter towards GOD and all that related to GOD. It spiraled downward over time as my spirit was fed by all the negativity on the news and the overall way the world was heading. I stopped putting up a Christmas tree the previous year. Not that the tree had any significance towards the birth of our LORD anyway but was more of a winter solstice thing.

The celebration of the birth of the Christ Child seemed futile in my mind. This was surprising to me as I recollected my past. I was raised a Catholic and attended parochial grade school. My parents always had a tree as well as a nativity set with fake snow material over stacked books to represent hills behind the manger. Scattered sheep and shepherds graced the hills while the wise men stood near the baby Jesus with their gifts. That's how my parents believed in their hearts it was supposed to be portrayed. Although, as I got older, I didn't buy into the snow around the manger. I guess it was a northeastern kind of thing. I had also come to realize that Jesus was born closer to mid-April rather than the winter solstice but such were the spiritual politics of the time.

Another day passed and I was feeling like I was on a roller coaster. Some days I was lifted up it seemed, doing the right thing while other days, I felt down in the pits for being self-centered. On those down days, I felt lighter than air, as if I might float away. It was the weirdest sensation and it bothered me. I hadn't been inside a church for some years, but I found myself stopping my car across the street from Saint Joseph's. As I approached, a three-legged dog barked at me from the alley. I made a slow walk up to the doors and opened them. Pausing for a moment, I decided to walk in. Entering into the heart of the church, I grabbed a pew and sat for a while. I put the kneeler down then got on my knees and prayed for some kind of understanding, as to what was taking place in me. A priest entered through a doorway near the side of the altar and knelt for a prayer at the front rail. When he stood, he noticed me near the back pews of the church. He made his way toward me, smiled, and asked if everything was OK. This was a very young priest. He asked if he could help in any way. I told him I was alright and just needed some quiet time. The priest let me know that he was nearby should I need anything. He then took his leave and retreated up to the altar, disappearing through the doorway from which he first appeared.

He probably went to call for assistance with a puzzled soul, I mused. Regaining my thoughts, I tossed around all that had happened recently inside my mind. I knew it all started that day in the mall when I first encountered the old lady. I needed to meet up with her and pick her brain.

Perhaps a hex or something was put on me, I mused. *No . . . that wasn't it. She was an odd but a kind spirit. I felt nothing but goodness in her.*

She knew more than what she was revealing. I ended up making several trips to the mall on Saturday with no success in finding her. Nowhere on earth did I loathe more than Saturday at the mall. Just insanely busy. I finally ran into her on Saturday night around 7 p.m. She wasn't in her usual place but rather down on the end of the mall sitting by one of the anchor stores. There were a few benches at that end which seemed to get little attention and she was the only resident when I arrived. She kept looking toward the double doors as if someone was going to meet her. Approaching her with a smile got me a warm offer to sit down next to her. She could see I was in a better mood than our last encounter. Today I felt composed and happy to be alive.

"Hello," I said, as I seated myself. "How have you been? You've been heavy on my mind."

"I bet," she exclaimed with a chuckle, as two shoppers passed by.

"Please tell me what's going on? I think I have a pretty good idea, but I'd like to hear it from you."

"So, you think you have an idea, hey? You see my friend, it is all based on spiritual enlightenment." I looked surprised! She continued, "What happens to souls once they become aware is that the body becomes buoyant to the gravitational forces of the planet. If the subject doesn't apply themselves in a healthy way, they virtually become a balloon. This will continue over time until one is whisked away for good. They refer to it as death. The choice is to start putting GOD's knowledge to good use."

"What do you mean by good use?" I countered, trying to pick her heart and mind.

"I mean good deeds without reward. It won't stop you from eventually dying but you'll be on the right path for living. Start applying your spiritual upbringing. Help those who need your help but don't honk your horn about all the good you have done. Keep it private between you and GOD. Give a listen to the mournful and let them know that there is a light that shines internally on all who seek it. You know what to do, you're just afraid. You are afraid to be a Mohammed or a Jesus or a Gandhi, but remember what the good book says: 'Blessed are the peacemakers: for they shall be called children of GOD.'[2] None of us are denied this gift. I believe you've had a few encounters these days that have shone you the way.

"We all reach that fork in GOD's Road. It is our choice which way we travel. There is great evil in the world which can sway the best of us into believing that their alternative path is the correct path. There is also great good in the world. It's all in the balance and it is up to us to keep it in balance."

She smiled a toothy smile and then calm came over her. Her eyes got soft, and she said, "When we first met there was a hole in you; an emptiness. That hole is slowing being healed."

---

2. Matthew 5:9 RSV

Suddenly her demeanor changed. She looked toward the entrance doors of the mall near the end of the corridor. A small gasp slipped from her lips and the door opened. A tall, thin man in a dark gray overcoat which had seen many winters walked slowly into the mall. He was bald with a dirty brown fringe around the crown of his head, which needed grooming. His hands looked dirty, and he needed a shave. He drooped like an under-watered plant when he walked. Black high-top sneakers on his feet beneath the tattered jeans and a black tee–shirt completed his portrait. I guessed him to be around forty years old, but I could have been wrong. When I turned to the old woman to ask her if she knew him, she had already re-moved herself and was fading down the mall corridor. When I returned my gaze to the stranger as he passed, he said, "What the hell are you looking at?"

I quickly replied, "Thought I knew you. I was wrong."

A chill went through me as I felt him as a dark presence. There was something off with this individual and I felt compelled to keep an eye on this odd creature. Removing myself from the bench, I moved towards the opposite side of aisle across from where I was sitting. At the same time, I kept the gray overcoat in my peripheral vision. He moved through the mall like a ghost of sorts, and I observed people around him give him space as if he were a leper. My overall impression was that this man was up to no good. It wasn't so much my observations of his looks and actions that brought me to that conclusion, but rather a deep feeling that he was not a decent human being. I had no facts to deal with. The truth is, he could have been having a bad day, but my gut told me that wasn't the case. Much like my encounter with the smelly guy and his friends a few days before, this one emitted a nonspiritual smell as well. If asked, I would have said, *He had a foul spirit or lack of grace.*

He walked up rather close to a couple of young girls in their teens, who were looking in the windows of a dress shop. When they took notice of him, he moved down the corridor following behind a mother and her young daughter. I made myself blend into the crowd as best as I could and after about twenty minutes of surveillance, I saw him exit the mall from the same way he came in. For the life of me, and I cannot figure out why, but I pursued. This guy gave me a cold chill. Walking briskly to the doors, I watched him get into an old, blue pickup truck. When he stepped on the brakes, I saw that the passenger side brake light was burned out. I turned and ran down to where I had parked my car. I could barely get the key in the ignition because of nerves and frustration. My car started and the chase was on. I almost hit a man in a silver corvette as I snaked around the mall road. He honked and I mouthed, I'm sorry! As I made my way around the back part of the mall where he would have been parked, I saw his one brake light. He turned right at the stop sign where mall lot exited to the main road.

I slowed my pace with the car as well as my mind, which was racing. The thought occurred to me that I was crazy for following this guy, but something was tugging me on. I wondered if it was just my active imagination. The pull was strong, and I needed to see where he was en route to.

Several blocks after leaving the mall he turned left and headed back into town. I followed like a hyena after a wounded gazelle, keeping a safe distance as not to let the creature bolt. Seven minutes later I found myself on the old side of town. The residential area had slowly turned into a slum over the years. Even the business area had succumbed to the liking of a ghost town. The city had plans for renovating this area, but it all took time and money. There was a right turn, off the road up ahead which led to a small park. After the park, the road continued to the new train terminal. The wind was blowing with a hint of snow as I turned at the terminal road. I saw his truck turn toward the access road, just past the new terminal parking lot. The old terminal was beyond there. I proceeded down to the parking area at the new station and parked my car. As I got out of my vehicle, I heard some tattered paper flap on the wooden telephone pole in front of me. When the wind blew it back against the pole, the part that remained said, "Missing: Faith." Hauntingly, it was a flyer I had come across all over town these past days and that my strange friend handed me.

Walking the service road which paralleled the tracks, I made my way toward where the old station was located. The city still hadn't razed the building yet and once again, the excuse was money. His taillight was faintly visible for a moment through the trees. It then went dark, and I assumed he stopped. My hands were cold and clammy. The distance from the new terminal parking lot to the old station was maybe less than two city blocks.

An odd thought crossed my mind . . . *no, it couldn't be. Was I being guided to . . . where . . . no, that would be just too crazy.*

I made my way down the road then moved through the small, wooded area that ran between the tracks and the access road. Tripping over some old junk, I fell flat on my face.

So much for stealth, were my thoughts.

Waiting a minute, I remained still to make sure I hadn't been heard. Standing, I looked around but all was quiet. I worked my way over to the main railroad spur that went directly to the abandoned terminal. I figured I could walk the ties and make less noise in my approach. As I neared the old station, I saw a light from a flashlight dance about within the confines of the building. Keeping low, I approached the windows of the old station, only to see the guy I was following slip back out the side door of the building. Hearing his truck door close and the engine start, I ducked low and waited until I heard the vehicle move down the road. It was late November and cold. It was only a couple of days before Thanksgiving, but I was sweating profusely.

I ended up returning to my car and followed this strange man to a house several blocks from the old train station. He parked his truck in the driveway then proceeded toward the rear of the building. I was a few houses down the street watching from my car when I saw the lights go on in the upper level. I assumed this was his residence. The outside of the house was in dire need of repairs. It could have used a coat of paint as well. After staking out his place for almost an hour, the lights went off upstairs. I waited another fifteen minutes for him to come back out. When he did not, I figured he had retired for the night.

Thinking things over, I decided to go back to the old station and find out what he was up to there. Signs were posted all around the building that read, "Condemned: No Admittance." It was like a calling card to anyone who didn't follow the law.

I entered the old train station through a broken door around the side of the building. It was the same door the odd guy had used to leave. Using the light on my cellphone, I panned the main area. There were the remains of a small indoor campfire someone had started in one corner of the waiting area where arrivals and departures accessed the trains. Assorted beer and soda cans dotted the building's interior, like jimmies on a donut. No doubt this was from some group of teenagers a while ago. They tended to party in these old, out of the way buildings or the adjacent woods.

This station had been shut down for about five years if I remembered correctly. Moving slowly across the main lobby I measured my steps, as there was a certain amount of debris on the floor. Broken beer bottles, a sneaker, junk food bags, cans, as well as boards and ceiling tiles were scattered everywhere. A few of the benches that were bolted down at one time were ripped from the floor and overturned. *Teen anger issues,* I gathered.

The ticket master's booth was near center, at the track side of the station. The windows were broken, and the counter looked like someone tried smashing it up. I walked past the bathrooms and kept walking, holding my breath. As I neared the far wall, I noticed two closed doors directly across from where the bathrooms were on the opposite end of the building. They once had signs on them, but the signs had been removed. All that remained were silhouettes of the plaques where they had been. As I approached the doors, I thought I heard weeping from the door on the right. I rattled the door, but it was secured with a new hasp and lock.

"Are you in there?" I called. "Faith, is that you?"

"Help me please! I'm scared! That man . . ." I heard in a tiny voice filled with tears. I looked around the floor for something to pry the door open with and when I couldn't find anything, I said, "Stand back away from the door! I'll get you out."

I took a running start and threw my body against the door. The door held. I looked around a second time inside the building for something to pry the lock off. There was nothing, so I took another body slam against the door. Adrenaline pumped into my being, and it started to give, so I hit it with all my might a third time.

Crack! The door sprung open splitting the wood with the lock and hasp attached. There in the small office was Faith. She crouched in the corner between a desk and the wall holding a pen-size flashlight between her bound hands. There were bags of chips, pretzels, cookies, and other snacks you'd find at the convenient store. Four sodas remained from a six-pack sitting in the opposite corner. There were two pillows, a twin-size air mattress, and two blankets. The young girl cowered at first.

"I'm here to help you, Faith," I explained. "Let's get out of here," I said in a calm voice as she moved toward me.

Suddenly, I heard a noise behind me. Before I could turn around, the pedophile planted a partial two by four hard across my back. It knocked the wind out of me as I fell to the floor. Faith ran back to her corner to stay clear of the altercation. The adrenaline kicked in again, and from my knees, I punched him right in the stomach. He swung the board a second time but missed as I ducked. Regaining my feet, I countered with a right upper cut which literally lifted him off the earth. I thought to myself, *He's not doing GOD's work, therefore he got lighter.* The poor child was screaming all through the fight.

Slamming my foot down on his chest, I knocked the wind out of him. That seemed to finish him temporarily. Grabbing Faith's hands, I managed to get the rope off of her, as we made our way to the new terminal. Ten minutes later we had the security guard checking out the old station. A 911 call to the police department brought reinforcements. The police responded quickly but the pedophile had run to his truck and left the scene. They police checked me out to make sure I was who I said I was. After the police interviewed Faith, she verified me coming to her rescue. I told the officers where this guy lived, as I had followed him earlier. They caught up to him and as they say, the rest was history.

I was told by the police not to make a habit of saving people but instead to call them. This was their polite way of saying there are enough superheroes.

The story was in the paper the following day. It seems that the pedophile had a record which stretched out over the years. The paper called me a hero, but I felt I was guided by something greater. In fact, I know I was! When asked how I knew, I told them the guy was driving erratically, which he was, so I followed him. When he pulled into the condemned train station, I thought it strange, so I continued to observe and follow this criminal. If I had told them of my encounters with the old woman, they might have locked me up!

Nine-year-old Faith was rejoined with her family. Afterward, the young girl was interviewed by child services to make sure nothing happened beyond being abducted.

Three days later after the news media had faded from my life, I returned to the mall in search of the old woman. She sat quietly on the original bench where we had first connected. As I approached, she held up the newspaper and said, "Man finds Faith! How interesting." And she laughed with that enlightened cackle of hers.

I blushed a bit as I sat down.

"How did you know?" I asked.

"I didn't," she said.

"I only went with what GOD guided me to do. The rest was up to you."

I looked into her eyes and said, "With everything that has happened, I never got your name."

Replying, she said, "You can call me Grace."

She stood up and gave me a hug, then looked down and said, "Your shoe is untied!"

"Oh yeah," I said, and bent down to tie it. When I stood up, she was gone. I never laid eyes on her again. Oh, from time to time I swear I feel her presence, especially when I forget who I am and start taking this world for granted. GOD's Grace.

The Cherub

CYN WAS NOT A bad daughter by any standard but just a troubled child of the millennium. A few minor mishaps had taken place in the past year from hanging with the wrong crowd. These occurrences, along with a pierced eyebrow, which infuriated her father, a dash of purple hair, and black lipstick, all gave way to a great level of parental frustration as each generation before has experienced. Cynthia's mother believed that it was just a stage that the girl was going through. That given time, it would eventually pass, and her daughter would find her way. Business had taken both of Cynthia's parents away during this week before Christmas. Rather than leaving her home alone where the opportunity for trouble could be a strong draw, they decided to send her to her grandmother's for a week. The thought of some old-fashioned bonding with the older generation might be just what the doctor ordered or so her father had believed.

Cyn just thought that it was a brainwashing experiment, and that grandma would be putting the "GOD rap" on her and how she should be a better Christian.

Cynthia was delivered to grandma's house in the middle of a snow squall. After a day of controlled silence and one word responses on the part of the granddaughter, things began to loosen up. Perhaps it was the smell of the bacon and eggs in the early morning hours, but there was something that took the edge off the wild child, allowing Cynthia to be herself in front of her grandmother. As the morning progressed, it was announced by grandma that the two of them would be making Christmas cookies a bit later in the day. At first this seemed like a bogus idea to the teenager but eventually Cynthia warmed to the challenge. Several hours after that, Cynthia left the kitchen where she had been helping with the making and baking of the Christmas cookies. With evidence of flour on her face and clothes, she nibbled on a sugar cookie. Walking into her grandmother's living room, she peered out the window and saw the new snow that had started to fall.

"Grandma! It's snowing again!"

Several inches of the white, fluffy stuff had already fallen a week earlier. Fall was being ushered out and the coming winter season had decided to make its second visible statement. This would be Cynthia's sixteenth Christmas and at that age, patience was indeed a virtue for those who had to deal with the teenager. Wanting Christmas to have happened yesterday, seemed to be most on Cynthia's wish list, not to mention the twenty or more items that she hoped for. She knew not to push for the diamond nose pin. That, and wanting to spend time with her new boyfriend, seemed to consume much of her thoughts.

Turning from the window, she noticed an ornament lying on the floor beneath the Christmas tree. As she walked over to replace it on the tree, she observed that it was broken at the top.

"Grandma, there's a damaged ornament out here."

"Just a minute child. I need to wash my hands."

A few minutes later, Cynthia's grandmother entered the living room and walked over to the tree to see what her granddaughter was holding.

"Oh no!" She said, "Not the Cherub!"

Taking the ornament from her granddaughter, she sat down in an overstuffed sofa. The top part of the handblown glass or neck of the ornament was broken. It was a small cherub in a flying position with wings spread. The piece was painted entirely in a bronze color. There was no bow and arrow, which would have been representative of cupid. The Cherub, nonetheless, with a faint smile on its face was no more. This was representative of one of GOD's celestial family. Today, it was a broken ornament.

Cynthia's grandmother's eyes welled up with tears as she looked at the two-and-one-half-inch keepsake. Her granddaughter saw this and, in her defense said, "Grandma, I didn't break it! I found it that way and we can get another one, I'm sure!"

"I know you didn't break it honey. It's just that this one was very special to me. It takes me back to a time when I was your age, maybe just a year younger, I think. I had just discovered that boys had another purpose on this earth other than to be irritating," the old woman explained with a half-smile, then she added, "It was also when I was shone that angels really are."

She wiped her eyes, then continued to speak, saying, "Come sit by me while I tell you a story that still makes me wonder sometimes, if I had imagined some of it or not. Like I said, it was many years ago. I was fifteen and just as pretty as a picture back then. There was this boy . . ."

As boys often fit a mold, Billy Montag was your typical teenage boy. The word "average" would not truly describe this boy. Standing at five foot, seven inches, he had a head full of brown, straight hair, which he combed with a part on the left. Brown eyes and a medium frame with no distinguishing marks, gave him much of an ordinary look. But the look was a disguise which disappeared when young Billy began to share his outlook on life with another individual. Neither introvert nor extrovert, nor athlete or slouch, left Billy somewhere in the middle of the pile. A thinker of sorts might be an accurate way to bring light to his nature. Still, he was neither an A student nor a struggler with his grades. Yes, a thinker! Perhaps a young philosopher would be a way to describe him . . . somewhere in the middle of the sages.

He preferred walking through alleys rather than taking the main streets, for it gave him an opportunity to see what was behind the storefronts and factories of his town. The young man had just recently put his bicycle away in preparation of the possibilities of driving a car somewhere in the coming year. It was the beginning struggles of leaving his childhood behind, while turning the corner on adolescence. Billy loved baseball, cars, and goofing around with his buddies. Collecting photographs of his favorite cars was a hobby with him and he had a few of his favorites on the wall of his bedroom. He collected articles that talked about the new and improved vehicles of the future. Billy liked to keep up with the coming changes for the new models.

Music was his other love. His taste in music varied. Billy was mainly interested in what pleased his ear rather than a certain category. He might focus on one type of sound for a while, then he would move on to explore other avenues of music.

On the spiritual side, Billy had been an altar boy since he was ten and pretty much had the run of the church, the parochial grade school, and parts of the rectory. He even knew where the door was that entered into the nuns' quarters, off the sacristy, behind the altar. It made access to the church quicker than walking around outside. It seemed like a secret passage from some old movie about haunted castles. All the buildings of Saint Joseph's were connected at some point, as much as a winter courtesy as anything else. This gave the appearance of a small community within the confines of a maze of buildings, and it was. The parish grounds were a second home to the boy. Billy knew how to get into the church from access of the rectory from the alley entrance. It gave him a feeling of clout. Billy went up the alley stairs and through the door, past the three-legged dog with one eye that Father Wei found living on the street. But that's another story.

The boy went down the stairs into the rectory's basement and onward through church basement and cafeteria. Finally, up the stairs on the other end of the school cafeteria and into the church vestibule.

There was a certain mystique to the part of the church that lay behind the altar. This was a spiritual place of a higher level in the boy's mind. Limited access was the priest's rule of thumb. The nuns had permission regarding the rear area of the altar and adjacent rooms, as they took proper care of the priests' vestments and the altar linens. The cleaning ladies who helped maintain the church's appearance were also allowed into this area.

Even though his altar boy days were almost over, for he was in high school now, he would help the priests out whenever asked. Billy was a good boy who always seemed to be on the edge of trouble's shore but never totally submersed in those rough seas. The silly kind of peer pressure stuff always seemed to get his attention, like throwing eggs, ringing doorbells, mild skirmishes on the playground during baseball games. He was cut out to be a boy with a future. When something did happen in his life that was not suitable behavior, such as the time he hit a passing bus with a snowball, it never happened again. There was nothing that a good scolding couldn't fix from an authoritative figure such as Father Joseph Folder. The boy kept one foot in the spiritual world of GOD and the church, while the other foot tested the waters of nonsense and stupidity.

Billy came from a family with one brother, Robert, who was four years his senior. Then there was Billy or William, as his mom called him. Adding his patient mother, completed the household of three. His father had passed away when he was two years old from an industrial accident, so the boy's memories were faint at best. Being raised by a single parent was a difficult task for any parent. His mother worked a full-time job at the local Macy's department store, where she made a decent living as the women's clothing manager. Being raised by a single parent might have added to the boy's minor explorations in testing life's water's but for the most part, Billy was a good but inquisitive human being.

Snow was falling in large flakes on this January day. The temperature was in the high teens and Billy was taking the alley short cut to the church. The boy went up the concrete steps and through the door. Billy avoided the rectory kitchen and slipped quietly into another connecting doorway. That, led down the stairs through the rectory basement, and into the cafeteria in the basement of the church. Father Wei's dog looked on with one eye from the top of the stairs watching the boy disappear. After eight years in the Catholic grade school, Billy knew his way around as well as any mouse that called the parish home. He continued through the church basement and up a spiral staircase that brought him to the vestibule of the church. He took a quick swipe with his hand at the holy water fountain then forward into the church. The young man genuflected, paying homage to GOD and making the sign of the cross. He slipped into the pew and said a short prayer for his mother, brother, and assorted relatives. Then he focused on a prayer for his father and got a bit misty-eyed. Finally, it was down to business.

"Dear GOD, I usually stand pretty much on my own and you know that from watching me, but I need your help on this. You see, there is this girl . . ." He paused for a long while. "I kind of like her LORD. Any help you might give me would be appreciated LORD. In the name of the Father, Son and Holy Spirit. Amen."

At the end of Billy's prayer, he rose to his feet. Leaving the pew, he genuflected in the isle and turned to leave the confines of the spiritual center he had come to know. He paused quickly, turning toward the alter and said aloud, "Oh yea, her name is Catherine!"

Continuing to exit, he dipped his fingers in the holy water, then stopped again. He got a prickly feeling up his back that he was being watched. Scanning the church for signs of one of the priests, he came up with nothing. He even thought it might be Lucky, the church mascot who got around pretty well on three legs. Billy knew the routine of the women who came in to dust and clean the altar. That was done on Tuesday and not a Saturday morning, so the boy felt it wasn't any of the cleaning crew. After a short pause, he shrugged his shoulders then continued on his way through the back of the church and down the street. Catherine's house was just a couple of blocks further up from Saint Joseph's and since he was in the area, it made perfect sense to take a walk by her residence.

She lived in a lower flat, near the middle of the block. It was painted yellow with white trim many years before. The house showed signs of pealing from the north's weather but that's not what brought him by the residence.

His pace was slow and deliberate as he prowled the neighborhood like a dog looking for a discarded bone. Even in his own mind, he wasn't quite sure what the attraction was to this girl, however, he was drawn like the moth to the blast furnace of hormonal change. Being an all-American boy, he tried to be on his best behavior, regardless of how his heart tugged away. GOD, country, and the pursuit of a caring but stern parent kept the boy on the up and up.

Slinking back and forth like a hyena, up and down the block several times, brought neither satisfaction to the boy nor any movement from Catherine's house. By this time Billy was beginning to feel like an idiot and decided that someone might have seen his odd behavior, so he headed down the street to the bowling alley. His older brother Bob was on a league, and it was always fun to hang around Bob's friends for a while. There was a hypnotic sound of the pins falling that gave Billy a good feeling, although he couldn't explain why. Maybe it was a musical connection to a drum roll. Placing a dollar on the bar, he ordered a Milky Way candy bar and looked down the bowling lanes for Bob and his teammates. When he spotted them on alley three, he moved down to the table that was behind the railing one step above the alleys. This made a great observation post.

Bob made eye contact with Billy after picking up a spare and said, "Hey, punk. Whatcha doing here?"

Billy just raised a hand in acknowledgment saying, "Killing time, just killing time."

"Well, wipe the chocolate off of your lip, kid," Bob countered, laughing.

Although Billy was there in the flesh, his mind was thinking about the sandy blond with the green eyes and the cute smile. Catherine stood shorter than Billy by maybe two inches. She had a very even disposition. One could call it almost serene at times. Still, if she were pushed far enough, her Irish heritage would come forth in the form of a storm hitting full force.

"Billy! Where are you at?" Bob shouted, getting his brother's attention. Bob then turned to one of his bowling buddies and explained, "The kid has that starry-eyed look. Must be after that girl, Catherine, I heard him talking about."

The two older boys started to laugh then continued with their game.

Billy gave them the buzz off sign and headed out the door. He returned up the block, making another pass down Catherine's street, but there was no Catherine visible. Nothing doing, he decided to return home and do what he was asked to do by his mother. He hated chores and cleaning his room was a pain in the butt, but disappointing his mom was difficult on him. He understood how hard she worked at her job, as well as how much time she invested into keeping the three of them together over the years. Remembering a teary speech from several years earlier on how both boys would have to help her keep things in order, he knew that his efforts were appreciated.

Within a few minutes time he was walking in the backdoor of their lower flat. He lived exactly six blocks down the street from Catherine's place, with the church falling halfway in between.

His room was a boy's bedroom that he shared with his older brother. There was an invisible line down the middle of the room. An old desk graced the center of the room, which separated the beds from each other, and gave the boys a homework station. The varnish was rubbed away from many years of use, but it was a strong piece of furniture with much character. Bob was there minimally, as he worked a part time job at the grocery store while he attended a technical college. His sole purpose with the room was to study and sleep. His schoolbooks were neatly stacked on one side of the desk with notebook and pen on top.

There was the typical clutter of a boy's room. Sort of an organized mess and yet it was not dirty but more spiced with each of the brother's personalities. Billy had a bookcase headboard, which displayed a variety of personal mementos from a small die cast Army tank to a pocketknife, and a Bible in black leather. A copy of *Call of the Wild* by Jack London leaned up against the Bible. There were a few additional artifacts scattered about the room, such as a bat, glove, and ball. There was an orphaned basketball peeking from beneath Bob's bed.

The curtains that hung halfway down the wall were beige and chocolate in color and made of a tweedy material. The bedspreads were a dark brown on Bob's bed, while a blue and brown stripe covered Billy's bed from pillow to foot. Hanging on the wall over the desk was a crucifix with dried palms slipped behind it from the previous Palm Sunday. There was a picture of their father nearer Bob's side of the room and a picture of their mother, which was hung on the wall on Billy's side. A few of Billy's favorite car images were taped to the wall. The walls were off white in color and a bit banged up from the boys. This was on their mother's list of things to do, which included a new paint job in her bedroom as well.

Billy worked on the room for about thirty-five minutes. He gathered up dirty clothes and straightened up the extra shoes. Getting everything else off the floor initiated the beginning of the challenge. Once that was done and the carpet was exposed, Billy got the vacuum out of the dining room closet. A quick run through with the vacuum cleaner and a boy's dusting of the most noticeable surfaces brought things to an end. About midway through the routine Billy started getting a queasy feeling. That began to slow him down, causing him not to put his all into the job. When he started to sweat, he thought it might be a good idea to call it quits. Needless to say, a few items found their way under the bed. Even though sick wasn't exactly the feeling he had but rather, very weak and a bit dizzy, he decided to lay down on his bed. After a few minutes, he drifted off to sleep.

"William. Hey, sleepy head," his mother tried to wake him gently, then kissed his forehead.

She had gotten home from work and found Billy sound asleep. About ninety minutes had passed since he dozed off.

"Huh . . . wah . . . ? Oh, Mom. Ahhee!" He mumbled and groaned as he stretched.

"Did you stay up too late again last night?" His mother questioned.

"No . . . just tired. Felt kinda shaky before."

"Hmmm," she offered, as she felt his forehead this time with her hand. But Billy was having none of it and was on his feet, ready to make a quick escape.

"I'm OK, Mom. Is the room good enough?"

"Well, it could always be better, but it'll do," she responded, as he was making his way through the hall into the kitchen, then in the direction of the backdoor.

"I'll see you later. I'm gonna head over to Mark's house and see what he's up to."

"Are you sure you are feeling all right?"

"Yes, Mom! I'm just a little tired is all. See you later!"

Billy went out the door and down the street. He started walking in the direction of his buddy's home. As best friends go, Mark was just that. They thought the same, enjoyed the same things, such as hoops, baseball, and cars, or just exploring the outlying neighborhoods.

Walking the railroad tracks was one of their favorite things to do. There was a fascination of checking out the backsides of buildings, such as manufacturing shops and small industry along the tracks. The tracks led to the river and bridges and so on, so there was an adventure highway for young boys and these two had traveled it for the past six years together.

But now, was the season of changes. Priorities shifted and other possibilities were now upon the horizon. Catherine was beaming brightly in Billy's mind, like the sun breaking the plain of night and presenting the miracle of dawn.

Finding his steps straying from a direct route to Mark's house, Billy started to feel the anticipation of maybe seeing the girl of his dreams. He went out of his way by a couple of city streets just to pass near her place. As he made the turn at the corner, he saw Catherine coming down the front stairs of her house. He hurried his pace down the sidewalk and when he was parallel from her but across the street, he looked up to catch a glimpse.

"Hi!" she said as their eyes made contact. This took Billy by surprise.

"Hi . . . hi, how are you, Catherine?" The boy replied in a loud voice.

"I'm OK. Just walking over to my girlfriend's house. You know Jean, don't you?"

"Yeah, I guess."

"Want to walk me over there?"

"Me? Real . . . ly . . . ah, sure, I suppose," Billy said, stumbling over his words. He crossed the street and smiled at Catherine as he matched her step for step. They moved down the street in an awkward way that two young individuals do when they are in the discovery mode. Kind of that looking down at the ground, toe-dragging walk, augmented with a darting glance every so often.

"What are you doing here Billy?"

"Huh? You just asked me to come over," He replied in a nervous but defensive manner.

"No silly. . . . What are you doing up in this area?" Catherine asked.

"Oh! I was just takin a walk over to Mark Shimski's house."

"Kind of out of the way, isn't it?" Catherine said with a smile, knowing that there were other reasons.

"Huh? Well, I guess," Billy replied, not really knowing what else to say.

They both walked the remaining two blocks without saying much of anything. "Nice day," comments from Catherine, followed by a grunt from Billy, were the extent of the exchange. It was difficult finding the right gears to engage and get the relationship underway. Upon reaching the house where Catherine's girlfriend lived, Billy stopped on the sidewalk. He watched as this special girl ascended the stairs to the front door. She turned and waved, again with that wonderful smile. Waving back with a quick arm gesture, Billy turned and moved down the street with the posture of a rejected soul at the gates of heaven.

I wish I could talk to her like in the movies, he thought. *I get eye to eye with her and I choke up. I feel so guilty looking at her breasts. I'm really sorry about that LORD but you made me like this. That's what Father Folder says. We are made in GOD's image.*

And so, Billy wrestled with his thoughts as he walked back toward his friend's house. It was late afternoon when he rang Mark's doorbell. He still was feeling a bit weak and queasy from earlier in the day, but he just put it behind him as a touch of the flu. Mark let him in, and they wasted the rest of the afternoon away talking about girls and sports. Billy called his mom to see if it was OK to eat supper at Mark's home and promised to be back by 7 p.m. He needed an early night, as he told Father that he would serve at 6 a.m. mass.

The alarm went off at 5 a.m. and Billy's hand danced under the covers until it found the opening. Hitting the button as quick as he could so not to wake his brother, Billy grabbed his clothes then showered and dressed in the bathroom. He took great care combing his hair in the mirror. A quick thought passed over his mind, as to when he first started to do this grooming routine.

When he was dressed, he turned out the light, then opened the bathroom door and slipped quietly into the kitchen. Grabbing a banana off the counter, he headed out the back door in the direction of Saint Joseph's. Billy made sure to bring along gloves. He wasn't a hat person because of the hair thing at his age but this day he was cold, so he did something he seldom did. He wore his Green Bay Packers knit hat and brought a comb along. Zipping up his winter coat was another thing that was never important to him, but this too started to become part of his routine. Recently, the cold weather was beginning to bother him. It seemed to work its way into his body, and he could never get warm. Billy had noticed that he was just feeling a little run down all together, even though he tried to hide it. Regardless, he had told Father that he would be at the church and the boy was a stickler about keeping his word. That was one thing about Billy's character: he always kept his word.

Entering from the alley side of the street, the boy spotted something moving near the rear door of the rectory, which was connected to the church. This was a cool shortcut if you knew the route through the maze of hallways and passages. As the boy drew closer, he recognized his friend.

"Grrr," was all he heard in the dim winter light as he reached the steps.

"Hello, Lucky! Are you guarding the parish grounds?" Billy greeted the church mascot, as the dog began to wag its tail in acknowledgement.

"You silly thing. You have more parts missing than not, but I appreciate your bravery. You're a good guard dog. Father Wei is lucky to have you."

The dog was a mass of scars, including a blind right eye. In addition, or better yet, maybe subtraction, the poor animal sported only three legs. The left front appendage was gone. Everyone affiliated with the parish took care of the unfortunate animal and in return the dog protected the church. This was the understanding of all concerned. A couple of years earlier, Father Wei found the dog in the city park. After a short discussion, the dog and Father reached an agreement and decided the church rectory would be a good place for Lucky to live. Everyone seemed to accept the animal as part of the church congregation, and we all felt a bit luckier. The church mascot made his home in the rectory but wandered the entire church grounds. Lucky was a light brown with some lighter areas, here and there. He weighed just over forty pounds and looked like he had been through hell.

Billy made his way inside the rectory and away from the cold weather with the dog following close behind him. Shutting the outside door, Billy pulled off the hat, then the gloves, and progressed down the stairs. The dog opted for a warm corner in one of the rectory's closets rather than follow. Lucky had several places to camp on the church grounds in consideration of his handicap.

The young man traveled through the rectory's basement then into the grade school cafeteria. Finally, up the stairs on the opposite end of the hall, brought Billy into the vestibule of the church. Billy made his way through the church to the priest's area behind the altar. Father wasn't there yet, which was good. This gave Billy the time to get set up for mass without additional pressure. The incense had to be placed in the burner; the brass chimes or bells needed to be positioned on the steps of the altar. The altar boy would ring them prior to communion, during the offering, and then again, later in the service.

Lastly, it was time to slip on the vestment, which was white in color and covered his shirt for the most part. Looking down, he realized that he had forgotten to shine his shoes, so he gave the tops a quick rub against his pants. The boy was prepared as usual with time to spare, so he took a walk down the aisle toward the entrance of the church to see if the doors were opened yet. Father had the key and would unlock the church doors about 6 a.m. First service was at 7 a.m. This would happen just before Father said his morning prayers. Unlocking early allowed access for the parishioners. Sadly, the parish had decided a few years back to lock GOD's house at night due to all the vandalism.

There was a stillness, a serenity in the early morning hours, with the first dawn's light filtering through the stained glass windows. It made it a good time to sit quietly and reflect before Mass.

The many rows of pews were of rich oak that was stained dark and had that look of having the knowledge of hearing many whispered prayers. The same oak was used throughout the church structure. There were magnificent beams that helped hold the roof in place and to Billy they looked like the ribs of the whale that Jonah had been swallowed by. Suspended from chains that were attached to the ceiling, were large wrought iron lights with stained bourbon colored glass that dimly illuminated the church. This added to the mystique of the old structure. About halfway down the aisle, Billy felt that odd sensation again, as if he was being watched. It was just as he had felt a day or two before but this time it was a bit more intense. He stopped in his tracks and looked around, as the chills climbed up his back.

"Who's there?!" He demanded but there was nothing. His voice bounced off the empty church and then, silence. The morning's sun rays passed through the stained glass windows, creating a kaleidoscope of colors on the interior of the church. Several patterns in blue, yellow, green, and red rested on Billy's face as he listened intently. Billy's eyes strained in their sockets and his ears were perked like a whitetail deer to locate some movement, something out of order, but all was quiet and peaceful inside the belly of the church. Walking the rest of the way to the vestibule, the teenager checked the doors. A slight push on one of the oak doors told the boy that they had been unlocked. *So, Father had been through earlier*, the boy deduced.

Billy considered, *Maybe there's a bum sleeping in the pews? Slipped in after Father returned to the rectory. It had happened before.*

He decided to move up the side isle of the church, past the statue of Saint Francis of Assisi. As he made progress towards the front of the church, he checked the pews on both sides of the aisle. He continued past a statue of Michael, the archangel. The piece was carved from white marble; its blank eyes looking down on the boy as he moved by. Each step brought him closer to the front of the church. Nothing or no one seemed to be around. Everything remained silent other than his footsteps. Just before his next step was planted on the floor, he heard the flutter of wings. It startled the boy enough to get him to jump backwards but he still could not see anything. Just about the time Billy was looking up and checking the rafters out in the church's upper structure, Father walked in. The boy stopped what he was doing and refocused on the things that needed his immediate attention.

Billy started up toward the front of the church. He genuflected in front of the altar, continuing through the opening toward the vestment rooms behind the altar. Just before he moved through the opening, he looked back into the large empty cavern of seats. He thought he heard someone giggle, but the church was empty with the exception Mrs. O'Conner, who had just entered through the same side door that Father had. She positioned herself in her normal place, on the end of pew 23. She was the widow woman who always attended 7 a.m. Mass. Appearing deep in her own thoughts, Billy dismissed her as a possibility. Continuing into the room behind the altar, the boy joined Father Folder in preparation.

Service went as methodical as breathing in and out. Father's sermon fell on the ears of about forty parishioners, who's attention varied from highly intent to almost asleep. He talked on forgiveness and how Christ on the cross, died for mankind's transgressions. Wondering if he himself had a clean slate with GOD, the boy said a short prayer. Billy's mind faded from the church service to thoughts about Catherine. Robotic moves got him to the end of the Mass. A thank you and a blessing from Father got Billy into the hallway moving toward the exit. Lucky stirred as Billy opened the final door that connected the parish to the alley. A low growl was followed by a look/see but the boy was down the steps, and on his way, while the dog was left to adjust back into a comfortable position.

CHAPTER 2

Catherine paused her conversation on the phone, as her mother moved through the dining room. She continued talking afterward with her best friend, Jean. It was late morning and a typical Sunday after church. With her folks finally occupied in the kitchen reading the paper over coffee and sweet rolls, Catherine had an opportunity to discuss love and life with her friend.

"I think he's cute but every time we try to talk to each other, he gets this odd way about him. He acts like he's angry about something, yet he doesn't say about what. He doesn't leave either but keeps staring at me," she said into the receiver.

"He's a boy. They think like rocks." Catherine heard the response through the receiver, and they giggled. Jean was a bit caustic because she had liked Billy at one time. Now that her interests were elsewhere, she had an *I don't care* attitude, rather than be overly supportive. Perhaps the coals of jealousy had gone cold?

"I heard that you were over by Colleen's house last week," Jean whined into the receiver.

"We did some homework together. Billy walked me over there that day. Just happened to be in the neighborhood," Catherine added with a smirk, knowing that Jean had an attitude growing.

"I don't know how you can stand her," Catherine's friend gouged back.

"Listen Jean, I don't care about that. I'm interested in Billy Montag."

"Sorry" was the response that came weakly through the receiver.

"I want him to talk to me, but I just don't how to get him started," Catherine continued.

"Just ask him about sports or church. He still seems to hang around the church even though he's in high school now and he always talked about baseball when I was letting him hang around me," Jean droned on, keeping Catherine's problem second to her own importance.

"Yeah, I guess you're right. I'll try to talk about the things that seem to hold his interest." Catherine responded, only half listening to Jean's subtle sarcasm. She just accepted her friend as is, with the hope that she would grow out of the bad habit.

"I wonder what he kisses like," slipped out of Catherine's mouth before she could think. Quickly she scanned the room for her mother who had the hearing of a German shepherd. Her body relaxing in the chair, gave notice that she was safe, and the comment had not been heard.

The two girls tossed opinions, dreams, and aspirations back and forth for about thirty minutes. After some concerned looks by her mother as she purposely walked through the room, Catherine decided that she needed to end the conversation. Farewells were exchanged and she hung up. Returning to her bedroom, she thought about Billy and Sunday seemed to drift away.

School started the next day and was no different than any other winter Monday. Homeroom was the watering hole where everyone met, and then it was off to classes. Catherine was a great student but between the bells it was all girl talk. At fifteen years old, boys were the topic of interest throughout the day but even more so when the bell rang. The dialogue was usually, how tall, how cute, how strong, and how smart.

The smell of meatloaf, mashed potatoes, and green beans filled the air. Lunch in the cafeteria was always the same with a regimented routine. Meatloaf on Mondays and fish on Fridays. Chef's surprise on Wednesday. The food was precisely measured out. No one received more than the next child. You entered from the left door in the hallway, moved through the line, as you picked up your tray and meal for the day. Topping it off with a carton of milk made the noon meal. It was then that you scurried for a seat, hopefully with a friend. This was the routine every day except for this day. On this Monday, Billy turned away from the end of the serving line and ran face-to-face into the girl of his dreams. Here she was, standing right in front of him.

Oh my GOD! I haven't talked to Catherine since that short walk to Jean's house. This is my chance, he thought. *I need to say something. GOD! Make something come out of my mouth!*

"Hi. Want to sit with me for lunch?" The words moved from behind his teeth before he could think.

"Yes Billy, I would. That would be very nice," Catherine answered with her signature smile.

Billy's eyes looked as if they were about to pop out of his head but somehow his body slipped into gear and they both moved toward the tables.

So far, so good, he thought.

Trays in hand, the two young hearts found a place to sit and began their first eye-to-eye conversation. It started out slow like cold syrup but once they got talking the syrup warmed up. Twenty minutes later, Catherine had agreed to meet Billy after Tuesday night devotions. He promised to walk her home if it was OK with her parents. The bell rang, and it was back to school business.

Tuesday night devotions were always a good reason to be able to get out of the house and the by-product was a bit of spirituality, thought young Billy.

Mrs. Montag was very proud of Billy and his involvement with being an altar boy. She believed that it gave the boy a good spiritual foundation that might help him later in life. Billy saw it as an opportunity to serve GOD by doing just a little extra. Escaping the home scene was a good adventure in the middle of the week too!

Getting to walk Catherine home after devotions was an added blessing, thought young Billy.

Father Folder was getting comfortable with several of the new altar boys but always enjoyed Billy's presence. Having Billy mentoring the new boys made the priest's job much easier. The boy was still in a slump physically and felt wiped out, but knowing that Catherine would be there in the church, lifted his spirits.

The middle of winter brought an early sunset, so Billy navigated by the streetlights. It was around six thirty with devotions starting at 7 p.m. The teen walked down the alley kicking a chunk of black frozen snow a passing car had left behind and repeated his moves pretty much the same as he had on Sunday morning. Lucky was nowhere to be seen but it was a large area to cover, and the dog was not one to just lie around. There were duties to perform as the church mascot and the dog took his role seriously.

Moving through the back door and down the steps that eventually led through the cafeteria, the young man moved like he was on a mission. The lighting was dim, as there were only some courtesy lights on to guide the way. Father was adamant about keeping the electric bill down. By no means did it give way to making the place look spooky, but when Billy heard the noise as he began to ascend the steps to the vestibule, the hairs on his back and neck stood at attention. He felt like he had just walked over a grave and a hand grabbed his leg.

The noise wasn't very loud, but it was there all the same. Hearing the flutter of wings put him somewhat at ease again as he reached the top of the stairs.

Must be a pigeon or two that got into the church somehow, he mused to himself.

As usual, Billy was earlier than he had to be, but he hated to be late and this gave him time once again, to set things up correctly for Father. Discarding his jacket, hat, and gloves, he took a quick look in the mirror the priests had in their dressing room. He wanted to make sure that his hair looked good and then put the finishing touches on his part of the service preparations. Being early had its other benefits and one benefit was that there was something very special about the church when it was empty. It was one on one with GOD. The boy could feel GOD's goodness and the spirit of the saints hung heavy in the air. The faint smell of the candles burning added to the spiritual side of things.

Once again, Billy heard the fluttering of feathers somewhere out in the body of the church yet, not the normal cooing of pigeons. Only silence. He moved slowly toward the doorway to the altar. Peeking around the corner, the boy scanned the vast open area in front of him leading to the pulpit. From his position by the side opening to the altar, everything looked normal. Never removing his eyes from the direction of the pews, he touched the holy water fountain and blessed himself. He saw nothing but the dimly lit ceiling lights as he scanned the church from left to right.

Walking out onto the altar steps he called, "Who's out there?" He waited a moment before calling out again, "Is there anyone?"

Only the quiet of the church answered back. The young man walked down the carpeted steps and around the altar railing. He began a slow walk down the aisle on the same side of the church he had searched on Sunday morning. Feeling a bit clammy, he staggered, partly because of his slow careful steps and because he was starting to feel poorly again. About half-way down the aisle, he paused and searched with his eyes the many places that a bird might be sitting up in the rafters.

From somewhere just behind him he heard a small giggle. This immediately spun him around where he stood eye to eye with a real, live cherub. It appeared to be small childlike creature with wings, who was in the second order of angels. The imp cast off the sweetest feelings Billy had ever felt. However, the shock of seeing this two-and-one-half-foot spiritual entity had Billy stumbling backwards, falling in between the pews. After landing on his back, Billy just laid on the floor in shock with his eyes extending from their sockets.

The little imp lifted himself off the top of the pew where it had been standing by the rapid movement of wings, then held a finger to its lips and said, "*Shhh!*"

At least the boy believed that is what he heard. The doors of the church opened and the first arrivals for devotions started to come in. The little guy started to rise in the air, giggled, and disappeared into the ceiling rafters, all the while Billy followed it with his eyes. In a mild state of shock with his mouth wide open, the boy remained lying on the floor unable to regain his composure. Processing this was taking a little time. One of the two people that entered the church was an elderly woman in her late seventies. She chose the aisle that Billy was in, and the teen could hear her feet shuffling toward the front third of the church where he was stuck like a turtle on its back. Trying to get to his feet, his hand slipped once on the kneeler, and he ended up on his back again as the old woman got to where he was struggling. She looked down at him indignantly and said, "Go home and sleep young man," then continued on her way to the front pew.

Billy, still in a state of shock, regained his feet and while walking backwards with his eyes scanning the rafters of the church, made his way to the altar steps. He paused for just a second, and then hurried into the room behind the altar, running right into Father Folder. "Easy Billy! You look like you just saw Saint Peter at the gates of heaven," Father commented, as the boy's eyes has a startled look about them. The priest held on to the boy's arm to help steady him.

"Huh?" Billy said, still with one eye looking out the door to the altar area.

"Sorry Father . . . I was startled by Mrs. Murphy."

Father Folder gave one of his looks where his eyes peered over the top of his glasses and said, "Let us prepare for devotions my boy."

The next minutes were spent getting the incense burner ready while Father got into his vestments. When all was in order, Billy lined up behind Father, who had chalice in hand, and they proceeded through the doorway. Service went as methodical as always but for the feeling of a burning sensation on the back of Billy Montag's neck. That uncomfortable feeling that one gets when one is being watched, gnawed on the boy. Every time Billy got up to move to his new position on the steps of the altar, his eyes went up to the rafters, searching for some evidence of what he believed he had seen. The end of the service was most memorable. Billy had caught sight of Catherine sitting in the side pew near the front of the church. The boy was all smiles, but his mind was still struggling with what had transpired earlier. As Father Folder led the way off the altar after the blessing, Billy looked toward Catherine, his eyes transfixed on her. Somehow, he misjudged his position and when he hit the step with his foot, he went down like tree being felled.

"Womp!"

The carpet muffled the sound of the boy hitting the floor, but a couple of snickers made their way from the pews to the ears of the priest, as well as Billy. The boy was vertical as quick as humanly possible and nodded to Father that he was all right as they moved off of the altar together.

"Did you hurt yourself, son? You seem to be at sorts with yourself. Is your health all right? You've been looking awfully tired lately," the priest questioned out of concern.

"I'm OK, Father . . . just was daydreaming . . . is all."

"Well, that's good Billy. You'd better get a good night's rest and thanks for your help tonight," Father added, as he closed the conversation.

Billy said goodnight and left via the altar, then down through the church's main aisle toward the front doors. He looked all around as he moved down the aisle wanting to call out to the apparition, but was afraid to make any noise because he thought that Father might hear him and in-vestigate. The boy was covered with goose bumps as he walked through the vestibule. When he made it out to the street, he saw Catherine waiting near the curb. She was just finishing up a conversation with her friend Jean. Upon seeing Billy exit from the church, Jean said goodnight and moved down the street in the direction of her house. Because of Billy's excitement, he was less standoffish and walked right up to Catherine, greeting her with a quick, nervous smile. Immediately following the smile, a worried look passed over his face.

"Hi."

"Hi yourself. Are you OK?" Catherine asked.

"Why? Do I look bad to you?" Billy countered.

"Oh! You mean about the fall! Yeah . . . I'm all right, just clumsy."

"Catherine . . . I saw someth . . ." Billy began to tell but stopped, then changed the subject.

"Let's walk, please," he said, as he quickly decided to move away from the church.

"Are you sure you are all right Billy?"

"Yes," he replied, as he looked back in the direction of the church, and then returned his eyes on his friend.

"Just a lot on my mind lately."

His friend shrugged her shoulders in a way that implied that she was not going to get anywhere with this line of questioning, so she stopped asking. They walked up the street towards Catherine's house and when they were within a block of it, Billy asked if they could walk a bit further. He needed more time with her but was not sure how to go about it, nor what he wanted to say or do. Somewhere along the main street where all the shops were, Billy reached out and grabbed Catherine's hand in a jerky but poetic approach. She accepted with a gentle smile that all but melted the young boy's heart. The couple walked glove in glove down the street, not saying a whole lot about anything but sharing their views in music, movies and what was their hardest class at school. An hour later, they finally ended up on Catherine's front porch.

"Well, I'll say goodnight. Guess I might see you tomorrow then?" Billy reached out with his words.

He stood there and she stood where she was but when she looked up at her front door to see if anyone was looking, the moment for intimacy passed. Although he wanted desperately to kiss his friend, he had no skills and opted to retreat. Turning quickly, Billy ran down the steps and disappeared into the cool winter night. Billy's mind was torn between thoughts of Catherine and his odd encounter in the church. The walk home was filled with quick looks over the shoulder as well as glances up at the trees and houses along the way. Half expecting the apparition to jump out at him at any time, a jittery Billy made his way through the neighborhood.

Although the remainder of his night was quiet, Billy's sleep was restless. His mind was working overtime trying to make sense out of what it was he saw. Did an angel, in fact, visit him, or had he imagined it all? At one point during the night Billy sat up in bed and said aloud, "A little angel, at that!" He quickly looked toward his brother who was sound asleep.

The next day was much like any other day and after a few days of the same strung together, Billy could only assume that he was a delusional teenager. Too many cookies and bad milk most likely were the cause of what Billy thought he saw that night. The following morning when Billy got out of bed, he noticed several bruises on both of his forearms. He took a look in the mirror while he was in the bathroom and was somewhat startled by the extent of what he saw."

Gee, I really didn't think I hit the floor that hard in church. Better be more careful and quit thinking about Catherine when I'm helping with mass, he thought. *Mom's gonna think I got in a fight. I better keep these covered up.*

Catherine's folks had slowed the romance down by setting her up with a Tuesday and Wednesday night babysitting job. This ended devotion's night and the long walks home afterwards. It wasn't that they didn't like Billy, but they saw the glitter in the young couple's eyes and felt space, along with time between them might cool the moment. It seemed to Catherine's Father, that Billy was showing up way too much around their house, then the devotions night, plus school, all added up to possible trouble. So, the new babysitting job broke up the week for the two teenagers. Weeks passed by between the two, with small encounters in the hallways of the high school. They couldn't get their agendas together. Billy would catch a glimpse of Catherine coming out of church each Sunday and then there were the walks that he took up to her house. Never really stopping, but rather just walking the street for a look, Billy would meander by to see if she was around. Being unsure of himself and at an age when a boy was torn between school, sports, his peers and suddenly girls, it was almost a pleasure to help his uncle out at the gas station. Feeling the pressure from Catherine's parents, as well as a few questioning glances by his mother, Billy just backed away from the relationship.

This was all new to the boy and he didn't understand that you needed to show interest or relationships would fade. After some weeks passed where there was little contact between them, Billy began to feel a great emptiness in his heart. He missed Catherine. Although he spent most of his time goofing around with his friends at the ice-skating rink in Washington Park, Billy still found his mind occupied with thoughts of her.

There was a beautiful frozen lagoon with two small footbridges that spanned over the water at separate places. It was a post card visual, complete with ice skaters of all ages and even a dog being pulled around on the ice by a young boy, or was it the other way around? A senior couple skated smoothly under one of the two bridges heading toward the north end of the frozen pond. Billy was at the rink with a couple of his friends on this cold day in early February. This happened to be the Saturday morning gathering place in the winter months, where everyone could let off a little steam by stretching their legs on a pair of skates.

On this morning, a short but intense snowball fight took place with the boys and ended with everyone being thirsty from the workout. So, as a light snow started to fall, the played-out group of winter enthusiasts decided it was hot chocolate time and headed for the boathouse.

Summer brought the rowboats out of storage, creating an atmosphere for romantic interludes upon the lagoon's waters, while the younger boys and girls went fishing for the big one. The lagoon was filled with stunted bluegills, carp, and sunfish. Although, there was the story of the two kids who caught a great big bass but that was years before. This did add to the folklore as well as created a fish that grew in size, as the years passed by.

Winter, on the other hand, brought out the hot dogs and hot chocolate at the snack bar inside the boathouse. The boats were neatly stacked at the opposite end of the boathouse. It also brought everyone up to the park to ice skate on the lagoon and the boathouse was converted into a place to change your ice skates, dry your gloves, and rest in between snowball fights. They would lay down a cork floor to walk on with your skates, so nobody slipped. The snack bar was a pleasant plus which provided a place to sit. Green movable benches once scattered throughout the park in the summertime, now resided inside the building. People took time to rest and chat for a while away from the elements, enjoying their refreshments.

Billy walked through the double doors, heading toward the refreshment stand. As he approached, he thought it was Catherine standing in one of the waiting lines and when she turned toward him, he smiled broadly.

"Hi!" he said with confidence.

"Billy!" she responded.

"I was just thinking about you. Why have you been ignoring me?"

"I didn't know I was. Guess with being busy and all . . . and, and working," he responded with some lame excuses. The truth was, he thought at times he was going crazy after seeing the Cherub in church. He kept this his own secret because he could not imagine anyone believing him. Distancing from everyone seemed like a good idea at the time.

"Hey! I was thinking of going to a movie," he quickly shouted out.

"Which one?" Catherine danced back.

"Oh . . . I don't know. I haven't really decided yet. Want to go with me?" he said with large eyes.

"Sure! That'll be great."

And so, the brief disruption by the parents trying to separate them, along with some minor nervousness which was easily overcome, gave way to a blossoming relationship called puppy love. The "meet me at the movies" here and "a walk" there became part of the ensuing weeks. Catherine and Billy became closer as spring entered the picture. It was a wonderful time of life for the two of them. Not only the discovery of who they were as individuals came into play, but also finding out who each other was. The likes and dislikes that two people have and where they both agreed, as well as disagreed with each other's thinking, helped paint the canvas of reality. Billy experienced some bad bouts with fatigue but pushed it off as just studying too hard. When this happened though, he would tend to distance himself from Catherine by explaining that he needed time around the house to help his mother out or that his uncle needed him at the service station last minute. He did notice that there seemed to be more bruises than he could explain away but he couldn't imagine where they were coming from, other than just banging himself up at his Uncle Harry's place by changing oil or taking out the garbage. He knew he was somewhat clumsy, but he always remembered the cause behind any cut or bruise and lately these seemed to just appear out of nowhere. His concerns faded at every new dawn and life started over each day with Catherine on his mind.

CHAPTER 3

Another movie had ended, and the two youngsters were in no hurry to get out of the theater. As if they were in a trance, they slowly moved up the aisle towards the exit. Most of the crowd walked around them to escape the confines of the movie house and get back to the reality of life. Young love was happy to hold hands. The teenagers could have cared less and lived at a much slower pace these days. The world around them truly did not exist. They moved in their own space, void of the reality that moved around them.

"What do you want to do now?" Billy inquired of Catherine.

"Well, I think you better walk me home before my parents start to worry too much."

"Yeah . . . I suppose you're right," he agreed, but not wholeheartedly.

Things were sweet in all areas of the boy's life however, there was this problem with seeing things, indescribable things. There were days that would pass by without an encounter of the celestial imp, while on other days Billy felt its presence, even if there was no visible contact. One night in May, Billy's radar was up. The teenage couple was walking back from an evening at the library. Billy swore to himself that the Cherub was close by. There was an itching sensation at the back of his neck and his eyes danced back and forth in his head. Catherine started to notice that Billy seemed fidgety. At first, she refrained from saying anything, but the poor boy was acting like he was wearing a wool suit with no underwear on.

"Billy! What's the matter with you? Do you have a rash or something?" the young lady inquired.

"No! I just thought we were being followed."

"Followed? By whom? By a bird?" she darted back.

"A bird?" he asked.

"Well . . . you keep looking up at the housetops, the trees, the sky, as well as down the street and behind us. You're not going to tell me you believe in superheroes, are you?"

"I'm sorry Catherine. If I tell you something, you won't think I am nuts, will you?" he questioned.

"I'm convinced you're nuts by the way you are acting right now. So, what is it? Do you see ghosts or something?" Catherine picked.

"Actually . . . I keep seeing a . . . a . . . little angel."

"Like your guardian angel, you mean?" she shot back.

"No, like a little cupid-type angel. It smiles at me. It giggles. It's driving me crazy. I know how this must sound but it's the truth!"

Billy continued to look around as they continued to walk. He scanned the area like a Marine checking out new terrain after making a beach landing. Even though he felt the little imp's presence, there was no evidence that it was around.

"Bill . . . I'm worried about you. You just haven't been yourself lately. Are you sure you are feeling OK?" Catherine asked the boy with great concern.

"I knew I shouldn't have had said anything. I figured that you would think I was off my rocker. You know, this goes all the way back to this past winter when I fell on the altar steps after devotions."

"Really?" The young girl said with surprise, as she visualized the incident in her mind.

"Yes . . . really," Billy restated.

"That was the very first time I saw it. It was before services, but I had felt its presence in the weeks before. It was weird but I knew I was being watched by something. At first, I thought there was a bum hiding in the church and using the pews for a place to sleep. Then that evening while getting ready for devotions, I was looking around for what I thought were pigeons in the rafters and it showed itself. It stood on the top of the pew and just smiled at me, and then it flew up toward the ceiling. If you'll remember after devotions, I came out of the church a bit startled."

"Yes, I remember now," Catherine replied, yet not entirely sure she remembered all of it.

The two young hearts continued their walk toward Catherine's house and cut down an alley, which would bring them up along the backside of her property. Twilight was settling in as they reached the gate to the backyard fence. Reaching the gate first, the young girl struggled with the latch. Billy waited a moment then said, "Here, let me do it."

"Let me do it," echoed in the air immediately after Billy finished talking.

The teenagers jumped in the air at the tiny sound behind them. When they focused, they both just stared in utter amazement as the little imp smiled, giggled, popped the gate open, then flew straight up in the air.

"Weeeeee!" Was all they both heard, as it faded into the night. Catherine plopped right down on the step after the gate, which was now opened. Her eyes were wide, and her mouth hung in disbelief.

"Billy . . . what did I just see?"

"Hey, you look like I imagined I looked that first night in church."

"Hey! You saw the Cherub too?!" Billy added with surprise.

"Cherub? Was that some kind of cupid or an angel of GOD?" Catherine uttered with a faraway look in her eyes.

"What does it want with you Billy?"

"I'm not exactly sure Catherine. I hope I'm not in trouble with GOD but then again, if I was, I would think he'd send a bigger angel."

They spent the next twenty minutes discussing what had just happened. Tossing ideas back and forth they decided it was some kind of miracle. Catherine would have it no other way. It was a miracle but for now she swore them both to secrecy. Deep down she believed she was cracking up but since they both saw the angelic creature, then how could that be? They both couldn't be crazy. The thought crossed her mind to talk to the priest in confession so it would remain a secret, but she discarded that idea. It was just too farfetched a thought at this point in time.

"I need to get in the house before my dad has a fit Billy."

"OK. Please let's keep this between us."

Leaning over toward the boy, she planted a small kiss on his lips and before he could react, she gave him the locked lips sign and ran through the yard to the back door of her house. A moment later Billy was alone as he worked his way down the alley. Whistling seemed appropriate, along with a hurried pace. His mind was split between the kiss and the happening with the celestial imp. The boy's eyes were everywhere as he made his way home, but his mind was in his heart.

When he was within three houses of his own house, he shouted out, "I know you're out there watching me but I'm not afraid of you!" He quickly darted up the street and into the confines of his home.

Several weeks had passed by since the incident with Catherine's first sighting of the Cherub. This was an early Saturday about 6 a.m., with the day looking to be a beautiful, sunny, late summer day. The birds were singing about the nice weather as the boy made his way up the street. Billy's uncle had asked him earlier in the week to work this morning at the gas station. The boy really liked chit-chatting with the customers, so it made for an interesting time in Billy's eyes, plus, he got paid for it. He started helping his uncle out when he was fourteen years old, doing odd jobs, like mopping the floors in the automotive bays and sweeping the office. He eventually graduated to more difficult chores like painting around the station, then finally pumping gas, changing oil, and washing cars. The boy was a natural talker, so the customers warmed up to him immediately. Uncle Harry's business was an old Mobil oil gas station, sporting the flying red horse logo as well as the red shingled, roof. The flying red horse sat high atop a pole with the gas price posted about halfway down the pole below the horse. There were those large changeable numbers, with the nine-tenths's of a penny always following the whole numbers, as to give the effect of a deal.

Walking along the sidewalk with his head looking down at the cracks, Billy observed the little things in life that a sixteen-year-old takes notice of. One of those was the dates embedded in the concrete sidewalk slabs, which told how long ago the concrete was poured. He also scanned the gutters for change. Up a nickel and three pennies, Billy approached the intersection where the gas station was located. When the boy crossed the street, he could see his Uncle Harry turning on the lights in the double bays where he worked on the automobiles. Other switches lit up the gas island as well as the office, the sign, and the bays. Looking up at the sign as it was illuminated gave the boy quite the surprise. Sitting on top of the flying, red horse was the Cherub. It waved at Billy and began to fly down toward the boy. Startled, Billy made a quick dash into the gas station's office.

"I'm here, Uncle!" he shouted at the top of his lungs.

"Yeah! I can hear you, as well as all the dead, sleeping in the cemetery Billy. They too can hear you," his uncle replied, grabbing his coffee cup.

"Sorry."

Billy turned around and peered out of the large front window in the office but could not see the little imp anywhere. His eyes were rolling around in his head like the silver balls on a pinball machine.

"Well?" his uncle asked, as he walked into the office from the automotive bays.

"Huh?"

"Did you come to work? Then get your coveralls on boy!"

As his uncle was speaking, the bell rang in the automobile bay area signaling that a car had just driven over the hose outside, which alerted the attendants that someone wanted gas. Billy struggled with the coveralls as he heard the car door close, and the customer's footsteps approach the station's office.

The door to the office opened, which caused the top of the door to break contact with a connection that was attached to the frame. This caused the buzzer to go off. In walked Mr. Edwards. Preoccupied and wearing a puzzled look on his face, he called out to Billy's uncle.

"Hey Harry, I need gas. Hey, have you ever seen a feather like this before?" He asked the boy's uncle, as he held the white feather up for all to see. It appeared to be translucent as well as iridescent. It measured almost thirteen inches long.

Billy's uncle took the feather from Mr. Edwards and looked it over. Then turned to Billy and said, "What do you make of that boy?" Holding the feather in Billy's direction as the three looked it over.

"Gee, I don't know! An eagle?!" Billy stammered, knowing too well that he had a good idea where the feather originated from.

"Well, then go fill up Mr. Edwards car and wash his windows too."

"Check my tires, would you Billy?" Mr. Edwards added.

"Yes sir," as he thought to himself, *there's two on each side, Mr. Edwards and they are still there.*

The two men continued to look the feather over and a few minutes later, came outside. They looked around in the trees across the street as well as searching the sky momentarily. Puzzled looks were there for a few moments as the men pondered. Billy returned to the men and announced that everything was taken care of on the vehicle, including checking the oil, which was fine. It was back to business as usual. Mr. Edwards gave the feather to Billy's uncle, paid for the gas, and then drove off.

The peace of the early morning had ended along with the feather mystery. Soon a stream of cars began to come into the service station for their needs, as the world slowly awakened. After a good hour of heavy customer traffic for gas, there was a short pause in the action. When Billy returned from the bathroom, he saw his uncle sitting at his desk, slowly twirling the feather in his hands. He wore a very puzzled look on his face as he examined it closely. When realizing that the boy was standing in front of him, he looked up and said, "You know, I've never, ever seen anything like this on any known bird. I've been an amateur bird watcher for years, but this is truly odd. I'll need to take this home and see what I can find out by checking some books I have."

"Yea, that's a good idea Uncle Harry. Beats me what it could be from. It may be a new breed of eagle," Billy added, then the driveway bell rang, and he returned to a waiting car outside. His motions were mechanical as he thought about what to do about the feather.

The next day found Billy sharing the feather story with Catherine and about what had happened at the gas station. Concern of this evidence had the boy worried, and he shared his thoughts with his sweetheart.

"Catherine, I need to get that feather away from my uncle. He might figure something out and then other people will get involved. There will be problems."

"I think you're worrying over nothing, Billy. How do you expect your uncle or anyone else to figure out that the feather is from a lower-class angel?"

"Shh! We don't want to insult the little imp," the boy responded, while searching the area with his eyes.

"I can't see how they could connect you with the feather, but I guess you're right, Billy. It's not something that should be in the hands of us mortals. Although the thought of stealing an angel's feather sounds terrible, it is for the right cause. We need to get it back to the owner. OK, what's the plan?" Catherine asked, with some renewed interest.

The plan was a simple breaking and entering but without breaking anything. They would need to wait until the following Sunday morning to put their plan in action. There was almost a week to nurture their ideas.

The days flew by for the two teenagers as they figured out different scenarios to approach their problem. Sunday morning seemed right for the job. Billy knew that his uncle went to noon service at his church, religiously. The plan was to sneak in through a window, grab the feather and slip back out of his uncle's house before Uncle Harry returned from service. The two teenagers met at Saint Joseph's that morning and after attending mass, they took a walk over to Billy's uncle's neighborhood. Using a couple of short cuts through a few neighbors' yards as well as an alley or two, got them to their destination.

After waiting for about twenty minutes, Catherine finally spotted Billy's uncle come to a stop at the corner. He made a left turn in his truck and pulled away in the direction of his church. Breaking into a quick run, the two teenagers on a mission, moved toward the bedroom side of Uncle Harry's house.

"Great!" Billy blurted out loud, when he found that the window was open a couple of inches. He slid the lower half of the window up and gave Catherine a hand, as he boosted her into Uncle Harry's bedroom. Billy followed quickly after her. It didn't take very long to locate the feather. It was sitting right on top of his uncle's dresser.

Billy picked it up and studied it in his hand as Catherine looked on. As she reached out to touch it, there was a swooshing sound at the window. In flew the Cherub and with one quick swoop, the imp did an aerial dive. It grabbed the feather out of the boy's hand as it exclaimed, *"Mine!"*

"You little devil, you!" Billy shouted as the Cherub flew by them and out of the bedroom window as quickly as he flew in. In a half of a second, the imp flew right back in again and landed abruptly in front of the boy.

It looked up at Billy and said, *"There's a little devil in all of us my friend, but GOD gives us choices."*

It smiled and, in an instant, it back looped into the air and was gone before either of the teenagers could spit out a response. The kids scrambled quickly after the celestial imp. They could not afford to get caught in Uncle Harry's house. The explanation would be just too wild for any imagination. Careful to leave everything just as it was, Catherine went out of the window first, followed by Billy. The boy returned the window to its previous position and the two sauntered down the street, careful not to run nor draw attention to themselves. Halfway down the block, they ducked between two houses, returning to the alley they had followed uptown.

Figuring that as long as the Cherub had its feather back, there was no need for the two of them to fret. Their first and only attempt at burglary ended on a peaceful note. The boy did wonder about the puzzled look that would soon appear on his uncle's face when he found the feather had disappeared, but it was out of his hands now and Billy just hoped he was never questioned about it.

Weeks passed quickly and in no time almost a season had gone by. Billy started to drift away from spending nearly as much time helping at the church with altar boy duties as he did. His mind and heart were filled with Catherine. Working part time at his uncle's gas station helped him treat her to the movies on occasion. Walks in the park were cheaper and fulfilling. Although Billy's Mom was somewhat lenient, she still made him bank half of his earnings, so he would understand the importance of saving for the future. She also tried to keep the relationship between the two teens limited in some respects, as did Catherine's parents, but it seemed to be a losing battle as they were sixteen going on seventeen. She wasn't prudent but didn't want her boy growing up too fast either.

Billy was on the move one, late, Saturday afternoon while pumping gas at his Uncle Harry's service station. He was starting back to the office to get the customer change from twenty dollars for the gasoline he had pumped. When he was within five steps of the front door, he was taken over with a clammy feeling and fainted, falling hard to the ground. When he awoke, Billy was in his uncle's truck moving toward the hospital. A lacerated, small bump now graced his forehead. Dizzy and feeling a bit sick to his stomach, Billy looked glassy eyed out of the side window of the truck. The houses moved by as metered marks to his fixed daze. With the hospital about three miles down the road, there was enough time to get into the rhythm of starting and stopping at the intersections. When they reached the last stoplight before the turn into the emergency entrance, something caught the boy's eye as he continued to stare out of the car window in a half daze.

His uncle was busy mumbling under his breath about the slow lights and traffic when Billy saw the celestial imp hovering in the passageway between the drugstore on the corner and the bakery next door. Again, the little creature appeared to giggle and hold its finger to its lips as a way of saying, "Hush!"

The boy turned quickly in the direction of his uncle to see if he too had seen the imp, but his uncle was looking straight ahead. Billy looked back toward the vacant space, which now existed and took a double take. Uncle Harry observed the boy's movement and asked without looking. "Are you OK, son?"

"Yea . . . just got a chill. What about the station, Uncle?"

"I locked it up," his uncle replied.

"Well, we're almost there. I think you'll be fine, but it doesn't hurt to check it out." And his uncle smiled, while he patted the boy's knee.

They checked Billy in at the admissions desk and about the time the paper chase was finished, Billy's mother arrived in the waiting room.

"Are you all right William? You're starting to scare me with the way you've been acting."

"I'm fine, Mom. Must have slipped . . . is all," the boy minimized.

Billy sat quietly as he waited for his turn. Finally, a nurse, who asked how he was feeling in deadpan, shuffled him into a room that was set up with a place for the gurney. The room was separated with a curtain, hung for privacy. A few minutes passed and a young doctor came in and said, "What seems to be the problem here?" as he took a look into Billy's eyes with a small pen sized flashlight.

"Look straight ahead for me," the doctor instructed.

"I took a spill at my uncle's gas station. Must have slipped or something."

After a few of the normal rubber hammer tests for response, along with following the index finger around the room, the doctor wrote a few things down on the clipboard. When he looked deep into each eye with the flashlight the physician seemed somewhat concerned. He turned to the nurse and said something about drawing blood after he noticed the bruising on the boy's arms. He also requested an ice pack for the boy's head.

The nurse returned in a few minutes' time with the ice pack and told Billy to hold it on his head. She seemed to be much friendlier now that they were away from the waiting area. By this time the doctor had said something about being more careful and that the nurse would finish up some tests, and to take care. Billy sat on the edge of the gurney, holding the ice pack against his head. He stared at the floor while listening to the hospital noises in the background. Maybe five minutes passed, and the nurse returned to draw the blood. She smiled at him and made a comment about good veins. Billy noticed her name on her name tag. It said Grace. The famous line "now, this won't hurt" was uttered and the blood vials were put on a tray. Grace left again.

Things seemed to quiet down, much like the lull in a conversation does, with several people all talking at the same time, then quiet. Billy continued to stare at the floor until he heard that odd sound again. There was that fluttering noise he heard at the church, followed by the privacy curtain moving. The boy sat straight up as the little head peered through the opening of the hanging curtain. The Cherub snuck in on the backside of the gurney.

"What are you? Am I dead or something?" the boy questioned.

"*Oh . . . no!*" It replied with great surprise and a joyful grin.

Billy slid down to the floor and stood there looking at this pleasant smiling, little, angelic imp. It reached up and touched Billy's fingers of his right hand and a warm surge ran through the boy's body.

"I like you," it remarked and slipped back through the slot in the curtains just as the nurse returned to tell Billy that he was finished and could leave. The boy stood there for a moment with a blank look on his face.

"Did you hear me son. We're all through," the nurse repeated.

"Huh? Yes . . . OK, I gotcha."

Billy staggered out of the area and searched for his uncle, who was waiting with the boy's mother around the next corner and down the hall. The doctor was walking away from the two adults as the boy approached. The boy's vacant look was not due to the bump but rather trying to comprehend what was going on between the doctor, his mom, and his uncle. The three of them followed the hallway past many doors, which led to the exit, while Billy's mother questioned the boy as to how he was feeling. She also added that they would get a call from the doctor if they found anything of concern but most likely they felt the boy passed out from exhaustion or because of a poor diet. Billy's eyes darted from left to right, checking out every corridor, every open door for some sign of the little angel. There was nothing. *I might be losing my mind,* the young boy thought.

Ten o'clock in the morning the following day, Billy was sitting in the kitchen. Contemplating a bowl of cereal, while probing it with his spoon, the boy sat quietly with a blank expression. He was told to just take it easy by the doctor who had been firm with his suggestion or so his mother had implied. The phone rang about four rings before Billy heard it. Finally returning to reality Billy got to his feet, walked over, and picked up the receiver.

"Hello?"

"Hi! Billy? How are you doing? I heard you hit your head yesterday," the voice on the other end said.

"Hi Catherine. Yeah, but I'm OK. I must have slipped or something. My uncle made a big deal out of nothing."

"Well, I just called to see how you were. I'm glad you're OK," Catherine replied, then she added, "You haven't seen the thing again, have you?"

Billy whispered in the phone for fear of his mother overhearing them. He responded saying, "Yes, at the hospital but for just a minute. I'll tell you later. Can't talk right now."

The boy then raised his voice and added, "Hey, thanks for caring! I appreciate it. I'm supposed to stay put today but I'll see you at school on Monday. Take care Catherine. Goodbye."

Billy hung up the phone, looked around to see if his mother was eavesdropping and when the coast was clear, he sat back down at the kitchen table. A small smile crossed his lips as he thought about Catherine. *She sure is great,* he mused.

By the time Monday morning rolled around, the teenager was ready for anything. Back to the normal routine, Billy rose out of bed, dressed, grabbed an apple, and headed out the door in the direction of the school. Moving at a teenager's pace, as if there were all the time in the world, the young boy made a slow but steady trek to the high school grounds. On the way past the bowling alley, he thought he heard the fluttering sound and jumped a little. After a quick look around, he realized it was only an exhaust fan from the meat market next door. School went as usual, except for Catherine being a bit too concerned for his well-being and picking his brain about the Cherub. After all, he was a man . . . of sorts. He could handle the bumps and bruises. He even felt he could handle whatever the little guy wanted. He had been praying every night to GOD to give him the "what's up" with what was going on with him. Billy wanted some assurance from the Almighty that he wasn't losing his mind.

After school, the boy started home by way of a couple of shortcuts. Teenagers never seem to have a direct route and since he didn't have to help at his uncle's gas station, he was safe to wander a bit.

Gee, I wish my head wasn't filled with all these questions, Billy mused.

"I need some answers, LORD!" He shouted at the sky.

Reaching the next street, Billy turned right and went down the alley. When he was about a third of the way down the alley, he turned right again. Billy was moving through a corridor between two buildings when the Cherub swooped down directly in front of him. The boy jumped backwards, almost to the point of leaving his sneakers behind. It took a few milliseconds to get his marbles back in order but when he did, the little creature was still there.

Billy struggled with the thought that he might truly be going out of his mind. Perhaps it was the expression or the feelings that the boy was emitting from his body, but the celestial imp moved nearer to the boy and rested his hand on the boy's forearm. A genuine peace washed over Billy. It was accompanied by a settling calm deep within. This let the boy know that everything was all right. It was the same as at the hospital.

"What did you just do to me?" Billy asked in a smooth steady voice.

"*I asked that the fear leave you,*" the Cherub replied in some form of telepathy, "and GOD granted my prayer."

"Oh! I see," Billy answered, not truly understanding but accepting the Cherub's answer, nonetheless.

"Hey! How did you do that?"

The Cherub simply smiled at the boy's question. "You are real! I thought I was just imagining all this. Of course, you would have to be real because Catherine saw you too!" Again, the imp was silent but pleasant.

"Wha . . . what's your story? Why do you keep following me? Did I do something wrong in church?"

Giggling, the Cherub fluttered its wings, rising into the air a couple of feet off the ground. Smiling at the boy, the little childlike creature explained through the thought method that it had started to use.

"*I need your help young Billy. I have been a Cherub for a long period of time that truly would be incomprehensible to you.*"

"Huh?" The boy remarked.

"*You wouldn't understand how long a time, is what I meant,*" the Cherub explained in simpler terms.

"*I have an opportunity to advance in the celestial ranks. There is a chance to move up to the level of angel. Part of my training is working with a mortal. I was allowed to choose from six subjects, and I found you to be the most appealing. The only question that remains is, if you are willing to work with me on a few issues that are important to GOD and the way of the spiritual world.*"

"Wow! This sounds like some heavy stuff. Hey, Cherub! You're not making any of this up, are you? This isn't about being some runaway Cherub who's done something wrong, is it?" Billy asked.

"*No, it is not. It's about changes Billy. For me it's about going from hmmm, second string to the varsity, to put it in terms you can make sense out of.*"

The boy stopped for a moment and looked around to see if anyone was observing him and the imp. Billy then returned his focus on the Cherub after he was satisfied that all was well.

"So, you want me to help you become an angel? This sounds like an old black and white Christmas movie," the teenager noted.

The Cherub remained in the air and smiled at the boy without making a response. Minutes passed as the two literally stared each other down. Finally, the boy shrugged and sighed, then said, "OK . . . I'll do it. If it's legitimate with GOD, I'll help you."

"*Good, Billy. You've made me very happy and yes, GOD is directing all of this.*"

CHAPTER 4

The weeks that followed were a strange time in Billy's life. Building a relationship with both, a celestial imp, as well as a friendship and his first romance with Catherine took its toll on the boy. Never in his entire life had he thought so much about so many things. Then there was school, as well as the family chores, and working at the gas station. The boy pushed himself with this full plate, as he had a genuine zest for life. This kept his busy agenda manageable most of the time. The ensuing weeks delivered a roller coaster ride with days of fatigue followed by spurts of energy.

An additional trip back to the hospital played into Billy's life as well. It seemed that the doctor couldn't quite pinpoint the cause of the problem, so a few more tests were in order. Billy wasn't concerned but rather annoyed that his life had to be disrupted. The doctor was a little strange as well, always peering over the top of his glasses and expressing himself with this low "hmmm" all the time, rather than saying any real words in front of Billy. Much of the time the doctor acted as if the boy were not a real person or like he wasn't even there in the room with him.

The conversations between Billy and the Cherub became much deeper of subject matter as time went on. The Cherub's mental telepathy or speaking aloud with giggles and all had Billy in an odd place. As strange as it seemed to the boy, there were many times the little imp acted like a small, spoiled brat who was full of mischief, and although the creature's nature was always pleasant, glimpses of sassy would peek out like the sun behind the clouds. It was as if the Cherub was as young as it appeared but at any time could tap into GOD's knowledge and share deep revelations with the boy.

Poor Mark, as well as many other friends' relationships suffered with Billy. Life has many changes, and the young boy was experiencing some major ones, with the biggest change of all to come. In the back of his mind, Billy thought there was a physical problem that was a bit more than the growing pains of adolescence, but he shoved those thoughts into a place where we all try to forget what our inner voice is sharing. In that, the boy was just the same as anyone and reacted in that common manner of denial. Life was laid out on a long table and Billy was there to pick and choose from all the dishes that were offered.

Father Folder had called Billy's house Saturday night and asked if the boy would serve at the 6 a.m. Mass that following Sunday morning. Father knew the boy was dependable for the early service. Agreeable as always, Billy said yes and decided to hit the pillow early. Morning came with sunrise still a ways off and with Billy already awake, he decided to get out of bed and begin the day. As the bathroom routine was in progress, Billy took a long look in the mirror. He looked at the dark circles under his eyes, which were enhanced by the pale skin surrounding them.

I look like a zombie, he thought.

A short shrug got him back into moving and within a few minutes the boy made his way down the stairs and out of the backdoor. Looking in all directions for his constant shadow, he believed the coast was clear and jogged down the driveway. It wasn't that the boy was trying to avoid the Cherub but rather it became a game of cat and mouse. Turning left, Billy continued up the street toward the parish church. Several minutes passed by and Billy stopped fast in his tracks.

"OK, I can feel you! Where are you hiding!?"

From out of nowhere the Cherub swooped down and landed right in front of the startled youth.

"Now cut that out! You're always surprising me," the boy told his new companion.

"We need to get going so I can get everything set up for Father."

"*I know!*" the imp said with a little chuckle.

"Now remember what I told you," Billy directed in a commanding way to the winged creature. "You can't be goofing around in church. Go find a nice place in the rafters and stay there quietly until mass is over with. I'm still puzzled at how you can talk so intelligently one minute and act like a three-year-old the next minute. I don't know where you learned to be so totally disruptive."

"*I mimic you!*" The Cherub said, quickly flying high near the lights that illuminated the alley below. Billy tried to follow with his eyes but the lights that were spaced along the back of the bowling alley blinded the boy temporarily.

"Mimic me?" the boy responded as he could feel himself getting flushed.

"Temper, temper!" the winged creature said, as he did a fly by.

"How do you figure that I act like that? Come down here where I can talk to you face to face."

The Cherub landed behind the boy and said, *"See what I mean? Just like a spoiled brat. Always demanding. Always looking to fill Billy's needs first and foremost."*

Billy jumped a little but had become used to these antics. Behind the boy, the first signs of dawn began to separate night from day.

"Well, you work me over then I get short tempered," the boy responded.

"The whole world acts like you do Billy. It's very sad to watch," the Cherub's voice was different now. It sounded more mature in Billy's mind.

"You all are given GOD's gift of life and from my perspective, you try desperately to destroy this gift by being unreasonable, by being cruel in the sense that, each individual wants his or her needs met first. Wonderfully enough, GOD would bless the soul who worries about his fellow man, who would share his last piece of bread with his friend and neighbor, or even more so, with his enemy. In this act, the enemy would perhaps become a friend. It is so simple and yet appears to be hidden in plain sight, right there, in front of each and every one of you. The people of this world have forgotten that they are souls first. That the body they walk about in, is no more than a physical vehicle for them to experience life on this level."

The boy sat briefly on the cement step in the alley behind the hardware store, absorbing all he had heard.

"You mean there is more than this? You mean heaven, right?"

The Cherub smiled. A quizzical look came over Billy just then and he asked, "But Cherub, what about all those people who are not Catholic? There are so many different religions. What happens to all those people?"

"That's a very deep question for one your age Billy but let me see if I can put it into perspective; a picture that might help you understand."

Then the Cherub looked down the alley at a figure of a man getting into his car. He was a third shift janitor who had just finished his shift. Turning to the boy the Cherub explained, *"Do you see that man getting into the Ford?"*

"Yes," the boy answered.

"Well, pretend that his car is of the Baptist religion. That other vehicle across the street is Protestant, another car is of the Islamic religion, and that Buick is the Catholic religion and so on. The man will get in his car to take him to his destination. If he got into a different car and drove to where he was going, would he not still arrive? This is how it is with GOD and the various religions. They are vehicles to get man to GOD, the ultimate destination."

"Wow! That's really deep! And no one gets it, do they? They all think they have the hot car," the boy responded with a half-smile.

At that, the Cherub giggled and flew up in the air, did a couple of loops and then left the boy to his thoughts. Billy continued over to the church. He was running a little behind after this philosophical talk, still, he thought about everything that had been said as he prepared for mass.

There is much more going on than we actually see, he thought. *It is comforting to know all these things though, even when it is told to you by a little celestial being.*

The boy thought about how good life was and how happy he was to be alive.

Summer took its place in the seasonal rotation. It was mid-July by this time and Billy had gone into the hospital for additional tests. During the past seven weeks, Billy had been poked and probed, with blood being drawn each time on three separate occasions. Going to the hospital was a big pain in the neck for the boy but he too, was becoming more and more concerned with his health. The last set of tests that had been administered were taken about eight days earlier. Poor Billy sported dark circles under his eyes and, without truly telling anyone, was feeling weak most of the time. He would go from periods of the sweats to feeling cold. It was as if he was fighting a flu virus that he just couldn't shake. Even though everyone the boy was close to felt there was something amiss, no one mentioned it aloud.

Billy's seventeenth birthday was nearing. He hoped it would be a great year, but his unknown health issue was constantly on his mind. Afraid to ask the Cherub, he kept his concerns to himself.

Dragging his tail, Billy came in through the kitchen door after working Friday evening at his uncle's service station. He found his mother blowing her nose in a tissue. Her eyes were red from crying.

"What's going on, Mom? Are you, all right?" the boy asked out of concern.

She looked up at him and beckoned the boy to her side. All she could do at the time, was to hug him and weep.

"Did somebody die, Mom?"

"No, William," she answered, choking out the words out.

After a few minutes had passed and she was able to compose herself, she looked up at the boy who stood steadfast by her side. Searching her heart and mind for just the right words seemed impossible, but she tried sorting through it anyway. Finally, she just started talking. "I received a call from your doctor today. They believe that they know why you seem to be so tired all the time, as well as the bruises. And the weakness and dizzy feelings that you have been having, this too is related. We need to have you go into the hospital for a bone marrow test. The doctor briefly explained to me what this procedure would entail. He said he would explain everything to you a bit more thoroughly at that time."

"What is it, Mom? You know what it is. Please tell me." The boy pleaded with his mother.

She looked up from the floor and said one word. "Leukemia! He thinks you have Leukemia."

"Leukemia? What's that?" Billy questioned.

A week after the bone marrow test, it was confirmed that Billy had acute lymphocytic leukemia. The mystery was finally over, and the culprit had been named. The boy thought to himself, *A fancy set of words that only said I might to die soon.*

The next two weeks that followed were much of a blur to young Billy Montag. He seemed to walk through his life in somewhat of a dream state. There was a period of strong disbelief by the boy, but it subsided in a short time. Finding out the finality of such an affliction was heartbreaking. There was the hope of a bone marrow transplant should a match be found. If it had not been for his contact and companionship with the Cherub, he might have reached a state of panic from which there was no return.

A remarkable maturity emitted from this young man who had just been given the worst news a human being can imagine. The realization that one's life has an expiration date. The doctor explained Billy's options and recommended chemo sessions. Knowing he was going to have to endure chemotherapy, he also knew he needed to talk to Catherine. He wanted to be the one to tell Catherine his unfortunate news. Try as he did to remain in a positive state of mind, Billy was feeling very low. This was supposed to be a high point in his life and what he had just come to learn was, that there was not much of a possible life remaining for him in the cards. All his future hopes and dreams of Catherine, life after high school, and everything else imaginable had just been taken away. He only had a short time left with his brother, or at least that's how it sounded. And then it occurred to him that he would be leaving his mother. She was the one who cared and nurtured him all the days of his short life.

Who would be there for her? Who would make sure that she took care of herself? his mind cried. *This just isn't fair GOD! I always tried to be good. I always was there for you. I know much worse behaved kids than me. Why? Why are you doing this?*

All these many questions flooded the boy's mind. Walking along the railroad tracks, eventually moving down to the banks of the Menomonee River, he pondered his existence. He thought of the friendships he had made, the teachers that had influenced his thinking and the many other mentors that had crossed his path. Thoughts of Christmas, trips to the northern part of his state, and autumn, were several of his favorite memories. These thoughts and other remembrances filled his mind. He continued his walk with a dejected look upon his face. The Cherub never left his side and kept quiet up to the time when Billy sat down on the ground and began to cry.

Sitting lightly on a large rock, the Cherub tried to explain some of the unexplainable realities of life as GOD knows it and not as man has tried to box it. No longer the celestial imp that the boy had come to love but more of a teacher, Billy listened intently and tried to comprehend as well as a sixteen-year-old boy could.

The Cherub began, "*I know that this is difficult for you Billy. You are so young in the mind's eye of a mortal. GOD knows your heart. GOD also knows your soul and your soul is GOD's business. Your time as Billy has been a time that has touched many other souls. They have come to know you and through you, have learned many lessons about their own souls. So many of these lessons were obvious, while others were subtle in their delivery. Everyone who lives in this form are part of a spiritual equation which is astronomical. Believe there are other forms, other planes of life and arenas of development in the spiritual, for there truly are. Beyond the things you might ever imagine, there are even more possibilities.*"

Billy nodded and blinked a couple of times in acknowledgement.

Continuing, the Cherub said, *"The leukemia that you have today will someday in the future be manageable in many cases and curable in others. You ask yourself why it is that GOD does not remove this burden, this malady from you, but if that was the case and if GOD intervened in all cases, you as a soul would never realize or rediscover who you were. All those souls affected by you would not learn their lessons as well and more so, they would not have an opportunity to realize who they truly are. The most terrible stigma that man has imposed on his self is to be under the belief that when one gives up the body, they die. This is the greatest falsehood of all because the reality is, one is born into a new existence. Just as an embryo is formed and develops into a baby when it reaches full term, the process continues by the mother giving birth. That baby then enters a new existence; a place completely foreign to what it has known. This is indeed what happens when we leave the body, as you know it."*

"Tell me how it is that you can look so silly and yet talk so intelligently?" Billy asked.

The Cherub simply smiled that pleasant smile that Billy had become accustomed to. Billy discovered, that in the silence that followed, the answer was often revealed.

"The scary part is I really understand you. Well, I guess it will make things a bit easier for me to explain to Catherine, now that I know a little more than a boy my age should know about what's going on with all of us people."

"And yet, you know very little of the wisdom of GOD's majesty," the Cherub added.

And so, Billy tried to absorb into his being the reality of what was approaching him. For one so young he handled himself in a most dignified way. Openly, he was not angry, nor did he blame GOD or anyone for what was happening to him. Rather, he looked for what good might still be accomplished. He wished to leave the world in a way that he would show GOD's strength in the shadow of death and transition. He also wanted to have some fun.

The boy felt better and wiped the tears from his cheeks. Standing, he stretched towards the sky, then without a second thought, he cuffed the Cherub playfully on the back of the head. The Cherub immediately went air born and double looped then rose out of sight.

"Come back you chicken!" Billy shouted with a small grin on his face.

The bantering between the two went on rather strongly during the next several weeks. This served as a good diversion for Billy and helped keep his mind off the future. The disease eventually took its toll on the boy's health in the year that followed. Now seventeen, he spiraled downward with his health. A failed bone marrow transplant darkened the days ahead. As the disease worsened over time, he had to be hospitalized. Young Billy had put up a valiant fight, but each man is somehow guided to his destination, one way or another.

CHAPTER 5

Hospitals always appear to be more of a place to repair and less a place of recovery. The greater percentage of recovery was done at home when deemed safe. But a much sadder story was unfolding in the terminal ward that Billy occupied. All avenues to recovery had been tried to stop the inevitable. He was not afraid, nor was he in a state of panic. Prepared mentally and spiritually for the transition, Billy merely waited for his loved ones to come make their final goodbyes. It was at this time after the supper dishes had been retrieved by housekeeping, when all was quiet and peaceful in the ward, when evening had settled to a calm, that the Cherub appeared for the last time. Billy heard the faint sound of the door open and close. The boy was staring out of the hospital window at the stars. He turned slowly toward the sound and upon seeing his small friend, he smiled and held out his hand. The little imp walked over, kissed the boy's hand, and then jumped up on the bed.

"I love you, Billy. GOD loves you. You're a brave soul, young Montag, and you've been a good friend as well. As I told you when we met, I needed your help. You did a very good job, Billy, and it showed me the beauty of the human spirit. I am allowed to move forward as you will do soon. It is my time as well. And thank you!"

Having said that, the Cherub flew a few feet away from Billy toward the center of the room. A strange mist surrounding a translucent membrane began to engulf the celestial imp. A faint hum was heard. Within, Billy could see what looked like some accelerated growth process going on. As multicolored light in gentle pastels moved through the celestial being you could see the Cherub's shape begin to change. After a few minutes the membrane dissipated, and before the boy stood a full-sized angel. There was a glow that did not compare to any description possible that a mortal might use. It literally gave off the power and love of Almighty GOD. Billy felt great comfort being this close to the angel and yet his mind struggled with what was happening to him. The boy was very weak and stirred briefly in the hospital bed. He had no color and blended into the bed sheets. The areas beneath his eyes were dark as if he had been lacking sleep for a long time. This was the only contrast to his features. The past month, food was difficult to hold down and there had been considerable weight loss. After adjusting himself in the bed, he looked in the direction of the angel and reached out for his friend.

"I'm afraid now."

The angel came close to his side and merely reached out touching the boy's hand. That gentle contact took the fear away as it had, not so very long ago after they met. A soft glow came over the boy and one could see the peace wash away all concern.

The angel smiled at the boy.

"I hope they remember me, dear friend. I will miss my first and only girlfriend. I will miss my family. I will miss everything . . . all the beauty of this world."

"*I know that this is difficult, Billy, but remember that what awaits you, will give way to a better understanding. You will begin to see things through GOD's eyes. I feel you will have company in a little bit. Your loved ones are coming to see you. I will be here, but you will not see me. You will feel my presence though, for I am to guide you on, my friend.*"

And so, the angel faded, as a mist fades among the morning light when the sun strengthens in the day. The boy lay still, reflecting on all that had transpired since first meeting the Cherub in the hollows of the church that wintry Tuesday night. The boy pondered, "*How GOD must love me, to send a tutor and companion, such as my nameless friend.*"

There was a soft knock on the door. It swung open slowly, bringing a weak image to the boy's line of sight. As Catherine got closer, Billy realized who it was. She was dressed in a powder blue dress. Her hair was pulled up and she had a few fresh daisies set in it. Billy thought about how lovely she looked. Try as he may to stay strong, several tears managed their way from the confines of his eyes. They followed the telltale trails down his cheeks.

"Hello Billy. I, I hope . . ." Catherine broke down and began to cry.

"It's just not fair. I'm so very sad for us Billy, so terribly sad for you. I've prayed and I've prayed but GOD must be angry with me."

"GOD's not angry with you or anyone else, Catherine. We're just not at GOD's level to understand all this. I've . . . thought, much of . . . this through, Catherine. It's going to be all right," Billy reassured her.

"Sure, it will Billy."

"Catherine."

"Yes, Billy?" she looked up, questioning.

"I love you. I wanted you to know that."

"I know . . . I love you too!"

At that point Catherine moved close to Billy, bent down, and kissed him lightly on the lips. Tears streaming down her face, she moved to a chair next to the hospital bed, sat down and continued to cry.

"It's OK my friend . . . it's OK," Billy said weakly then closed his eyes to rest. A few minutes later the door opened once again and it was Billy's mother, accompanied by his brother and uncle. His uncle approached the boy, bent down, kissed his forehead and roughed his hair slightly.

"How you doing Billy?"

Billy opened his eyes and smiled.

"I'm all right Uncle Harry. Doing just fine," the boy replied, although everyone knew it was not so.

Uncle Harry placed his hand temporarily on the boy's shoulder, giving it a slight tap of assurance. He then moved over to a place against the wall, pulled out a handkerchief and blew his nose. Billy's brother Bob was the next to approach the hospital bed.

"Hey, Billy, . . . I, I'm sorry Billy. I'm sorry for every mean thing I ever did to you," Bob choked out the words through the tears pouring down his face, then continued saying, "This just isn't right. You never did anyone any harm. I just don't get it."

Billy's Mother moved closer to Bob and rubbed his back, at which time Bob moved away from the bed.

"How's my brave boy?" She said with reddened eyes but held back the tears hoping it would help the situation. She took hold of his hand and rested her other hand on top of it.

"I'm doing good Mom, just very tired. I love you, Mom," young Billy said and he closed his eyes for the last time.

"It was some months after the funeral, when I was visiting Billy's grave," Cynthia's Grandmother explained. "I'd go and place a small bouquet of flowers there, you know. One day as I bent down to put the flowers in the small black vase that was there, I saw it sitting on the lower edge of the headstone. It was just there. I got a weird shiver down my spine like I was being watched. Then there was a calm feeling that came over me, and I knew that everything was all right. I just knew. I picked the feather up and slipped it inside my coat. It was shortly after that day that I was shopping for the holidays and spied the little Cherub ornament in a store window, hanging on a display tree. I brought it home with me. Every Christmas since Billy's passing, I have had that ornament on my tree, my dear. I truly had not spoken about any of this to anyone in all these years. I thought, who would believe me? But, as GOD is my witness, I saw the little Cherub. I know there are angels just as I know there is GOD."

Placing the ornament on a shelf near the tree, the old woman sighed. Catherine then turned to her granddaughter, hugged, and kissed her. They returned to the kitchen to make up another batch of Christmas cookies. A few minutes passed and Cynthia said, "That was a really good story, Grandma. You should write these stories down."

"What? Do you think that I made that all up child?"

"Well . . . didn't you?" Cynthia replied with her hand on her hip.

"Just a minute, Granddaughter. I'll be right back."

The old woman disappeared down the hallway and into the bedroom. A couple of minutes passed by and when she returned, she held in her hand a remarkably iridescent, yet translucent feather that measured approximately thirteen inches. The young girl stood there with pie sized eyes and her mouth wide open.

"Grandma, it's beautiful!" The tears began to stream down Cynthia's face and her countenance softened, as she gave her grandmother a real hug.

For Mary, New Beginnings

Bibliography

W., Bill. *Alcoholics Anonymous*. 3rd ed. New York: Alcoholics Anonymous World Services, 1976.

Watts, Isaac, and George Frederick Handel. "Joy to the World." In *Christmas Music Companion Fact Book*, by Dale V. Nobbman, 24. Anaheim Hills, CA: Centerstream, 2000.

www.ingramcontent.com/pod-product-compliance
Lightning Source LLC
Chambersburg PA
CBHW072004170626
46813CB00005B/2010